Coldhearted
HEIR

USA TODAY BESTSELLING AUTHOR
MICHELLE HEARD

Cover Designer: Sybil Wilson, PopKitty Design

Cover Model: FOREST

Photographer Credit: Wander Book Club Photography

TABLE OF CONTENTS

Dedication

To my readers.

I adore you.

Songlist

Coldhearted Heir available on my playlists on *Spotify*

Synopsis

Everything changed the night my boyfriend died. What should've been the most special moment of my life turned into a nightmare. Because of Hunter Chargill, I lost the love of my life. I'll never forgive him.

Hunter used to be one of my best friends, but it turns out he's nothing more than an arrogant a-hole determined to make my life a living hell with his lies. But he should've known you can't break something that's already broken.

I manage to avoid him until my freshman year at Trinity Academy. Our cruel words and intimidating touches quickly spark a flame, and instead of us going down in a blaze of hatred, desire sizzles to life.

I know I'm in trouble when I start enjoying our fights. Instead of wanting to punch him, I find myself wondering what his lips would feel like on mine.

A stupid game.

One kiss.

And my perfectly constructed walls come crashing down around me.

I should feel guilty and make Hunter pay for what he's done.

But sometimes a tormentor turns out to be a protector.

Coldhearted Heir

THE HEIRS
Book 1

College/New Adult series of interconnected
STANDALONES.

"We do not merely destroy our enemies; we change them."

— **George Orwell, 1984**

Family Tree

HUNTER CHARGILL

↓   ↓

Mason Chargill   Kingsley Hunt
Father   *Mother*
                      (Nickname: Hunt)

Godmother: Layla Shepard

Godfathers: Falcon Reyes & Lake Cutler

Best Friends: Jase Reyes, Kao Reed & Noah West

JADE DANIELS

↓   ↓

Rhett Daniels   Evie Cole
Father   *Mother*
                      ↓
                      Hayden Cole
                      Grandfather

Godmother: Miss Sebastian

Godfather: Carter Hayes

Best friends: Fallon Reyes, Mila West & Hana Cutler

Jade Daniels fell in love
Jade Daniels lost it all
All the king's horses, and all the king's men
couldn't put Jade back together again.

Chapter 1

JADE

Two Years Ago...

I stop packing for a moment and lift my burning eyes to my friends. They spent the night at my house and have been trying to convince me to stay. "If I don't go, I'll end up starting a war. It's only for the rest of the long weekend."

Jase's birthday party was a disaster, and I need time to process it all before school on Tuesday. My grandfather's ranch has always been a safe haven for me.

Fallon gets up from the bed and moving closer to me, she takes hold of my hand. Her golden-brown hair is still a mess, and her soft brown eyes hold a world of

11

understanding as she says, "You're hurting right now. Running to your grandfather's ranch won't make anything better. Call Hunter and talk to him."

Anger coats the disappointment swirling in my chest. My vision blurs, and my throat aches from all the effort it's taking not to cry. I swallow hard and take a deep breath before the words come out, thick with hurt and anger. "If I could, I'd move to Virginia for good. Brady is ignoring my calls, and I never want to see Hunter again."

Fallon looks to our friends for help. Mila rises from where she's sitting on the floor amongst the scattered blankets and pillows, we used for the sleepover. "Jade, we've been a tight-knitted group since birth. Hunter was only looking out for you. Any of the guys would've done the same thing. Hunter was just the first to react. You know how protective they are of us."

Shaking my head, I have to swallow hard to get the lump down. "Last night was supposed to be a special night for me. Hunter ruined it all." I let out a harsh breath. "He embarrassed Brady in front of all our friends." My shoulders slump as a wave of disappointment and sadness washes over me. "He humiliated me." I pull my hand free from Fallon's and reach for another shirt. Folding it, I voice my worry, "Lord only knows what happened between them when Hunter took Brady home."

Hana stretches her body across the bed so she can reach the side table to grab her phone. "That's it. I'm calling Hunter. We need to settle this ASAP."

"Don't!" Before I can continue objecting, my own phone begins to ring. Knowing the ringtone belongs to Brady, I almost break my neck when I jump over my luggage to get to the device before it can go to voicemail. "Brady!"

Breathless, I wait for his voice to come over the line.

"It's me. Colton." Hearing his voice makes a frown rumple my forehead.

This can't be good. Is Brady so mad at me that he got his older brother to tell me we're over?

Colton's voice sounds numb as he says, "Things got bad last night."

I fist my free hand next to my side as I stare at the wall in front of me. "Let me talk to Brady." I need a chance to save our relationship. We've been dating for a year, and he's been one of my best friends since the first day we started school.

We can't end like this.

"Colton, we need to leave right now!" Hearing the panic in their mother's voice makes my frown deepen.

"I'm coming," Colton yells harshly before turning his attention back to our call. "Brady killed himself."

Shock and confusion numb me, and it prevents the words from sinking in.

"Wh-what?" My mouth dries up, and my heart starts to beat faster.

"I have to go."

The line goes dead. My hand drops from my ear, and my eyes creep to the phone in time to watch the screen go black. Silence stretches around me, making the air thin as my breathing speeds up.

"What did he say?" Fallon asks.

"I - I – I." Unable to form the words, a wild panic bleeds through my body when what Colton just said begins to sink in.

No.

I shake my head and drop my phone as if it might burn me.

"Jade?" Mila comes to stand next to me, and I see the concern on my cousin's face.

I hear a knock at my bedroom door, and it takes a lot of effort to turn my face toward it.

Daddy peeks inside. "We're ready when you are." His eyes meet mine, and that's all it takes for the finality of Colton's words to hit.

"Daddy," I croak, and my breaths start to hitch in my throat, making it tighten with pain.

"Bean?" Dad rushes forward and takes hold of my shoulder, worry darkening his features.

"Brady…" I choke on a sob, and my eyes flood with tears. Denial wars with the harsh reality I'm struggling to face. My voice is strained, making my throat cramp as I force the words out. "Brady killed himself." I grab hold of my father's arm, needing to hold on to the strongest thing I have as the full force of what's happening hits me. "He… he's dead."

Dad's arms fold around me, holding me tightly to his chest, and it keeps the pieces of me from shattering to the furthest corners of the world.

"I'm so sorry, Little Bean," Dad whispers as he presses a kiss to my temple.

I begin to gasp from the pain searing through me. It's tragic and relentless, not giving me a second to catch my breath. "Daddy." My voice is torn between a wail and something hopeless.

Keeping his promise he made on my fourteenth birthday, Dad moves his arms under me and lifting me up, he walks us to the bed where he sits down and cradles me. *'I promise to always be right behind you, Jade. So I can catch you when you fall and hold you up when life gets hard.'*

Right now, Dad's the only thing holding me up as my world distorts into something unrecognizable.

"Girls, give us a moment alone," he orders my friends to leave. When the bedroom door shuts behind them, Dad frames my face and lifts it until our eyes lock. "I'm here, Jade. I know you're hurting so fucking much, but I'm here, and I won't let go."

My body begins to jerk as the sobs rip through me, and I crumble in my father's arms.

Brady's gone.

Every dream I wove around us fragments into tiny pieces.

My Brady.

My best friend.

The love of my life.

He's gone.

I won't get to hug him again.

I won't get to kiss him.

I won't get to see his gentle smile that had a way of warming the coldest days.

Brady's dead.

My sensitive, beautiful boyfriend left without warning, without a word… and he took my whole heart with him.

———————————

My world has been a warped and hollow mess the past couple of days. For the first time since I was a toddler, I slept in my parents' bed. They haven't left my side since I got the news that Brady committed suicide.

Mom called Mrs. Lawson to find out where the funeral will be held so I could be there.

Sitting between my parents, my eyes keep drifting between the closed casket and the front row where Mrs. Lawson and Colton are seated. Even though it's almost summer, the church is cold.

For a fleeting moment, I wonder where Mr. Lawson is. But it's a constant fight to keep it together and to focus on anything. When Dad lifts his arm and places it around my shoulders, I scoot closer to him. He puts his free hand over both of mine, and warmth seeps through the ice barrier coating my skin.

My stomach burns, and my back aches from all the tension. I try to concentrate on the physical pain because facing the merciless devastation inside me is too much to handle right now.

I don't think I'll ever be able to face it.

When the service starts, my mind becomes a torture chamber filled with questions, denial, and sorrow.

Our time together wasn't long enough. We were never meant to say goodbye.

A tear rolls down my cheek, and I don't have the strength to wipe it away. Mom frees a tissue from the stash she brought and gently dabs the trail away.

The turmoil in my head is so loud, it drowns out all the sounds around me. The preacher's lips move. Mrs. Lawson's shoulders shake. People get up and sing, and I lean heavily against Dad to keep myself standing.

When the service comes to a close, we make our way to the exit. Stopping in front of Mrs. Lawson and Colton, I somehow manage to force a smile around my dry lips. Their faces blur as I unconsciously pay my respects. "I'm so sorry." I blink the tears away, and immediately I'm struck by the anger and pain in Colton's eyes.

This must be so hard for him.

Another fleeting thought as Dad guides me out of the building toward the car. The only constant in my world is the tormenting reality that Brady is gone.

We follow the procession to the cemetery, and even though the sun is shining bright, the grounds feel dark and morbid.

Brady doesn't belong here.

Brady was sweet and caring. He was sensitive and gentle and doesn't belong in such a grim place.

Beside me lays a single poppy, and I notice it's already wilting. It was Brady's favorite. When we come to a stop near the gravesite, I carefully take hold of the stem, so I don't accidentally break the flower.

As I walk toward the already forming crowd, my eyes dart over the gravestones, and each one is a blow to my broken heart.

I'm not ready to say goodbye!

Dad must feel my distress because his arm is around my shoulders before another tear can escape, and he whispers, "I wish I could take your pain, Little Bean."

I cower against my father's side as the preacher says some final words, and the coffin is lowered into the hole.

Brady can't be in there.

But he is. He's dead and never coming back to me.

The tidal wave robs me of my breath and makes my heart squeeze so painfully, I wonder how it's still able to beat.

People begin to leave, having said their final goodbye. I force myself forward, and Dad sticks to my side as I kiss the frail petals of the poppy before dropping it on the coffin.

An agonizing sob tears a hole right through my soul as I croak, "I'll love you forever, Brady."

I somehow manage to turn to Mrs. Lawson and Colton and weakly wave at them before Dad helps me back to the car.

It's only been three days, and I've barely survived the heartache. How am I going to survive the rest of my life without Brady?

It all sinks in again.

The pain. Feeling lost. The desperation that's threatening to cripple me.

Every second between each heartbeat is unbearable because it's another second without him.

Dad called the school and managed to get me out two weeks early before summer break, so instead of heading home after the funeral, we all came to Virginia.

I'm sitting on a bench, my eyes staring blankly over the little pond on the ranch. It's beautiful and peaceful out here, but right now, I can't bring myself to appreciate any of it.

I hear footsteps, and then a shadow falls over me before Grandpa sits next to me.

"Hey, kiddo."

I link my arm through his and holding onto it, I snuggle into his side, resting my head on his shoulder. "Hey, Gramps."

We sit in silence for a while before I ask the question that's been weighing heaviest on me, "Why did he do it?"

"He must've been in a place so dark he couldn't find the light."

I need to talk to someone about the mess in my heart, and Grandpa is the wisest person I know. He's a retired Navy Seal, and I'm sure he's seen the dark side of life a couple of times.

"We were happy together. There was an incident at Jase's party, and Hunter embarrassed Brady. I don't know what happened when Hunter took Brady home. Colton,

Brady's older brother, said things got bad, and that's why Brady committed suicide."

Grandpa lets out a heavy breath before he asks, "Did Hunter and Brady fight?"

"I don't have the heart to ask Colton what happened, and I don't want to talk to Hunter."

"So, you don't actually know what happened?"

I sit up and scowl at the water. "I can only guess, Gramps. It was serious enough to make Brady feel like he had no other choice."

Grandpa rubs a hand over his strong jaw, his brows drawn together. "I think you should call Hunter and hear what happened. From my experience, a lot has to happen before someone reaches the point where they feel like death is the only option."

Deep in thought over what Grandpa said, I nod slightly.

"Dinner is almost ready. Want me to put your plate in the microwave until you're ready to eat?"

Sometimes I think my grandpa and dad know me better than I know myself. Smiling gratefully at him, I nod. "Please. I want to stay out here a little while longer."

Grandpa pats my knee before he gets up to walk back to the house. For a while, I watch the last of the sunset before I pull my phone from my pocket. The screen lights up, and right away, my eyes focus on Brady's smiling face. The blow is so hard it reduces me to a crying mess in seconds.

Clenching the phone to my chest, I startle when it begins to ring. Seeing Fallon's name, I croak, "Hi."

"How are you?" There's only a second's pause, then she rambles, "Don't answer that stupid question. I just want you to know I'm here for you. I wish I could hug you."

Hearing my friend's voice makes the tears start again. "It's just hard. I can't wrap my mind around it all. One second we're happy, and the next, it feels like I've been thrown into a horror movie."

"We love you, Jade!" Mila's yell comes over the line, followed by Hana's, "and we miss you."

My friends manage to bring a faint smile to my lips. "I miss you too. I just need to process everything."

"You're coming back after the summer, right?" Fallon asks.

"Yeah, my parents won't let me stay here."

Fallon clears her throat, and her tone sounds awkward when she asks, "Have you spoken to Hunter? He's been trying to get a hold of you. When he asked if you're okay because you're not answering his calls, I didn't know what to say."

My anger has taken a back seat because the grief was hard enough to deal with. "I'm just sorting through the mess in my mind before I take his call."

"Are you talking to Jade?" I hear Noah ask, which means my friends must be at Mila's house. Noah and Mila's fathers are twins, and the two families always spend a lot of time together.

Before Fallon can answer him, Noah takes the phone from her, and the next second, his voice comes over the line. "Bean, are you okay? The girls said you're in Virginia."

"Hey, Noah."

Things happen fast over the next couple of seconds. I hear Kao, Jase, and Hunter in the background, and then the call is switched to video, and I'm staring at Noah's worried brown eyes.

"Move to a spot with light so we can see you," Noah instructs, and like a robot, I listen. I get up, and when I reach the first lamp that lights up the path back to the house, Noah grins at me. "That's better. How are you holding up?"

Kao's face pops into the screen from over Noah's shoulder, and he gives me a caring smile.

As the words start to form on my lips, Noah holds the phone in the air so everyone can squeeze in around him. The moment I see Hunter, anger and heartache swirls in my chest until it feels like my insides are nothing but a bloody mess.

Distraught, I shake my head and cut the call.

I can't do this. I can't face Hunter yet.

Everything is still too raw.

My phone begins to ring again, and seeing Hunter's name, the betrayal and hurt I've been suppressing wins out, and my voice drips with rage as I answer, "Don't ever call me again. You lost that right when Brady killed himself because of you. I hate you, Hunter Chargill." A sob cuts through my voice, but I force the words out, "I hate you, and I wish it was you instead of Brady. What did you do to him?" My emotions spiral out of control, and my voice climbs with hysterics as I scream, "What the hell did you do to Brady?"

"Jade, I didn't do anything." The confusion in Hunter's voice only infuriates me even more.

I can't believe he's playing the innocent act right now!

"I don't believe you!" I suck in a breath of air and bring my free hand to my clammy forehead. "I'll never forgive you, Hunter. Someday I'm going to make you pay. I don't know how or when, but I promise you, you'll pay for what you've done to Brady."

I cut the call and let out a scream as I throw my phone into the darkness. My breaths are coming too fast, and it feels like I'm not getting any air in. I let out another scream and start to sink to my knees, but before they can slam against the cobblestone pathway, Grandpa appears out of the darkness and grabs hold of me.

Taking hold of my trembling hand, he presses it against his chest and locks eyes with me. "Just focus on my breaths, Jade." The first couple of breaths are painful as if I'm coming up for air after drowning. "Deep in. Let it out," Gramps keep repeating until my breathing evens out.

When he's sure I'm okay, his arms wrap around me, and he holds me tightly. "Let the pain in, Jade. I'll be here to put you back together."

My voice is muffled against his chest. "It hurts too much."

"I know, Jade. I know." I hear the faint echo of loss in his voice, and it feels like I'm bonding with my grandfather on a deeper level — a level where only the darkest pain lives.

I let out a scream that's stifled by his shirt before I cry for everything I've lost.

Every dream. Every kiss. Every touch. Every day of the empty future stretching before me.

Because of Hunter, I lost the love of my life. I'll never forgive him.

Chapter 2

JADE

Present.

Hunter 22; Jade 18

My grandfather once told me every time you drop to your knees, it's a chance to push yourself harder. You do whatever you have to do to keep going. You never give up.

After I lost Brady, I spent every chance I got on the ranch with Grandpa. Whenever I visited him, I didn't have to pretend I was okay. Instead, Grandpa and his best friend, Uncle Max, gave me an outlet for my pain and anger by teaching me how to fight.

They said I have to fight until the fire inside of me is nothing but dead ashes scattered over the bodies of my enemies.

I only have one enemy.

Hunter Chargill.

I thought I could avoid him. I even tried convincing Dad to let me go to the rival college instead of Trinity Academy, but he wouldn't hear anything about it. Unfortunately for me, Dad is friends and business partners with Mr. Chargill, Hunter's dad, who's the president of Trinity.

Unless I tell Dad the real reason why I want to change schools, but I can't do that. I never told Dad it was Hunter's fault Brady committed suicide. Only Grandpa knows. This war is between Hunter and me, and I won't drag our fathers into it.

So here I am, staring up at The Hope Diamond building I'll be calling home for the next four years.

Luckily Hunter is a senior, and I only have to survive one year without killing him. I'm not sure it's possible, though.

HUNTER

Just like my father, I took a year off after school before starting with my studies, and I'm regretting it for the first time. Had I started at the academy right after school, I would've been done, and wouldn't have to face a year of living with Jade.

I walk through the shared space where our living room and the kitchen are. The suites were renovated not too long ago, and the new smell still lingers in the air. There used to be only three bedrooms in the penthouse suite, but after the extensive makeover, there are ten rooms that take up the entire space of the top two floors of The Hope Diamond building. It's the main dorm on campus. The Pink Star and The Oppenheimer Blue are situated across from our building. Depending on where your family's wealth and status ranks, you're allocated a suite in the relevant dorm.

My great grandfather and his two best friends created Trinity Academy and CRC Holdings, where I'll be taking over as President in a couple of years. It places me at the top of the food chain alongside Jase, Fallon, and Hana.

Being one of the crowned princes at Trinity has its ups and downs. Every girl wants your attention, and every guy wants to be your friend or challenge you.

Fallon steps out of one of the suites, and her brown eyes land on me. A smile forms around her mouth. She's grown into a beautiful woman. I'll probably have my hands full this year, keeping all the horny fuckers away from my girls.

When I'm sure she's alone, and I don't have to get ready for a fight with Jade, I ask, "Still moving in?"

Everyone knows Jade hates me with a passion that has a nuclear capacity to blow up whenever we're in the same room.

"Yeah." She glances around, then asks, "Have you seen my lazy cousin?"

"Jase?" I shake my head. "Last I spoke with him, he said he'd be here in time for classes."

Jase, my best friend and one of the crowned princes, will take over as CEO from his father in a couple of years. We grew up close and might as well be twins.

Fallon shakes her head, her hair falling over her shoulder from the movement. A loving smile takes the sting from her words as she says, "God help us and CRC when we start there. We'll probably work our assess off to make up for Jase not doing his work."

"Yeah." I chuckle, but it fades when Jade comes out of the room that's opposite mine.

Fuck.

Her ginger hair shimmers in the electric light. There are auburn strands I haven't noticed before. Fewer freckles are sprinkled over her nose than she used to have. After the disastrous incident, I haven't seen much of Jade. I heard she spent her summer breaks on her grandfather's ranch, and I get a feeling she did it to avoid being around me.

We might not get along, but I'd be blind not to notice how fucking beautiful she's become. There's a pang of sadness and resentment when I remember how close we used to be.

After her boyfriend, Brady, committed suicide, I tried to find out why Jade blamed me, but after two years of this shit, I've given up. Now I just roll with the punches.

Jade's brown eyes land on me, and they instantly darken to black with the anger that always bubbles to surface when we come face to face.

"This is going to be one hell of a long year," she grumbles as she gives me a look I've grown accustomed to seeing on her face — a mixture between hatred and pain.

"We can call a truce. At least it will be a bearable year then," I offer.

Jade stares at me until the air grows thick with the hostility she feels for me. Slowly shaking her head, she says, "There will never be a truce between us, Chargill. Not while you're still breathing."

"Jade." Fallon's voice is soft and cautious.

Jade glares at me for a moment longer, then she turns her face to Fallon. "Let me know when he's either sleeping or out. I'll finish unpacking then."

Without another glance in my direction, Jade heads for the front door, and a moment later, it slams shut behind her.

"Hunter." Fallon gives me a pleading look. "This needs to stop."

I let out a sigh and go after Jade. Our friends are growing tired of the war between Jade and me.

Fuck, I'm tired of this shit. A person can only take so much, and the fact that I'm being blamed for something I didn't do is grinding at my soul.

Yeah, I admit I might have overreacted at Jase's party two years ago. But damn, Jade was only sixteen, and the thought of her and Brady having sex had me losing my mind.

I yank the front door open and shout after her, "Hold up, *Little Bean*." I know using her childhood nickname will have her exploding.

"Are you looking to die today?" she growls as she swings back to face me.

The corner of my mouth lifts in a grin. "Love life too much. We need to talk and settle this thing once and for all."

"You think it's that easy to get away with murder?"

Not this again.

"Would it make you feel better if I let you beat me up?" I ask, reaching the end of my rope with this woman.

She doesn't hesitate to answer, "It would."

Hearing she's dead serious, I shake my head. "Not gonna happen."

"Pussy," she chuckles darkly.

"Calling me names won't help shit," I bite out, aggravated that it's so easy for Jade to disrespect me.

"Fight me, Chargill," she snarls. Moving closer, she seems ten fucking feet tall even though she barely reaches my shoulder.

She stops when her body is only a couple of inches away from mine. All it would take for me to put her in her place is to lean down and claim her downturned lips.

What. The. Fuck?

Where did that come from?

All this fighting must be fucking with my head but not able to resist, I do lean down an inch, and I watch as her eyes narrow more. I stare into her simmering black gaze while a slow smirk pulls at the corner of my mouth.

"Never took you for the kinky kind, *Little Bean*."

Her breathing begins to speed up, and it makes her chest brush against mine with every inhale. Her features set into hard lines, and then she lets out a cruel laugh.

Pretty sure my family jewels are in danger right about now.

Our past together has taught me when Jade laughs instead of cries, I'm in deep shit.

"Fucking coward," she hisses.

Thank God for survival instincts. Just in time, I take a step to the side and closer to Jade. Her knee comes up and slams against the outside of my thigh. My hand shoots out, and I grab hold of the back of Jade's neck, yanking her so close I can taste the lingering mint on her breath.

"Careful, *Little Bean*." My voice is low, tainted with the loss of our friendship and my own rage because Jade keeps blaming me for something I didn't do. "Your outbursts are growing tiresome. I'm only holding back because of our fathers."

Not backing down, there's murder in her glare. "I'm done caring what our fathers would think. Go to hell, Chargill."

Shaking my head, I smirk at her. "You don't seem to realize," I tighten my grip on the back of her neck, and my eyes turn icy with a look I inherited from my father. Tilting my head, I lean so close her eyes widen. Just before our lips touch, I let my mouth skim over her cheek until I reach her ear and whisper, "I am hell."

Her scent has changed.

Instead of the sweet-smelling deodorant she used two years ago, I get a lung full of something soft and fresh.

Staring down at Jade, I take in her features. How's it possible she's changed so much? There's no sign of the sixteen-year-old who used to be my best friend.

In front of me stands a woman, devastatingly beautiful. She's become coldhearted and vicious.

I have to admire Jade for her spirit as she reaches up and grabbing hold of my wrist, her nails sink into my skin. I let her pull my hand away from her neck as the familiar look of loathing settles on her face.

Hey, at least one thing hasn't changed, right?

"I'll never back down, so you better be prepared for war because I don't intend to lose."

I stare at Jade and slowly shake my head. "*Little Bean*, didn't your grandfather teach you there are no winners in war?"

Deciding to abort the peace-seeking mission that turned to shit real fast, I yank my arm free from Jade's hold and stalk back to the suite.

Slamming the door shut behind me, I glare at a wide-eyed Fallon. "Fuck knows why I still try."

Fallon walks over to me and wraps her arms around my waist, pressing her cheek to my chest. "I'm sorry. I wish I could help."

She's one of the few people I allow to hug me freely. Fallon and Hana are the daughters of my parent's best friends, the Cutlers and Reyes'. Our families are inseparable and loyal to a fault.

Wrapping my arms around her, I let out a tormented sigh.

"I'm not gonna lie. This thing with Jade is eating away at me. I'm at a total loss."

Fallon pulls back and giving me a careful smile, she asks, "Have you tried beating her with kindness?"

I let out a burst of laughter. "I seriously don't think that's going to work."

I've been staying in my room so Jade can get settled without running into me. I shouldn't give a fuck whether she's uncomfortable with me here, but I do.

Frustration mixes with the memories of our lost friendship. I can't stop loving Jade the way she stopped caring about me. It's not that easy.

Our friendship must've meant more to me than it did to her.

Needing a distraction, I open my playlist on my phone and turn up the volume when *Love The Way You Lie* starts to play.

I let the angry lyrics wash over me, and hurt and frustration boil to the surface. Wanting Jade to know how I feel about this fucking war, I yank my door open. Jase, who was just about to pass by my room to get to his own, freezes like a deer caught in headlights.

Jade yanks her door open, and glares at me, her breaths already rushing over her parted lips.

"Oh," Jase says as he takes a couple of steps backward. "Fuck."

Keeping my eyes locked on Jade, I can see heartache mixing with the anger on her face, and I know the lyrics are getting through to her. I'm totally taking it as a win.

My eyes don't leave hers as the song ends. I lift my phone and press stop, but Jade makes a show of looking at her own phone, and soon a song starts to play. The words are drenched in pain as they drift to me.

And I listen. I force myself to stay rooted, my eyes glued to Jade's while the words lash at me. *Praying.* The fucking song hurts, tearing my already fucked up heart to shreds, but I don't back away. This is the longest we've been in the same space since *that* night.

Hearing just how much Jade is hurting is sobering and tormenting. I always thought we'd somehow be able to work through this, but now I'm not so sure.

Where do I even begin to get past the walls she's put up between us?

The song is a clear fuck you. Jade has no intention of ever being friends with me again.

When her song ends, I press play on *Too Good At Goodbyes.* I hope she listens to the lyrics the way I listen to hers. If this is the only way we can talk, then so be it.

Jase ducks low and rushes past our rooms. Before he disappears into his bedroom, he mumbles, "Fun times."

As Jase takes refuge, other doors around us open, and our friends peek out of their rooms.

"They're finally communicating," Mila whispers to Fallon.

While the lyrics drift around us, I silently beg Jade, *'Don't think I'm heartless or cold. I don't want to say goodbye. I still want to mean something to you. But fuck,*

39

you keep hurting me, and I'm only human. I'm scared the time will come where I can't take anymore, and it will really mean the end of us.'

I can't tell whether Jade can hear what I'm trying to say until she presses play on another song. *Yeah, it's going to be another soul-destroyer. She doesn't care about what I want or how I feel.*

The words *You Broke Me First* cuts right through me. I can see Jade is affected in the same way, and her raw pain screaming from her eyes is a blow that almost takes me to my knees.

I don't choose another song, which has Jade continuing her torture session by playing another gut-punching song. It's angrier than the first two, and I notice how the pain in her eyes dims as rage takes its place.

Crossing my arms, I lean against the door jamb while the tension keeps building. I don't miss how Jade's breaths keep coming faster.

I hate seeing her like this.

When *I'm Not Afraid* starts, Jade's body tenses. After a couple of seconds, her anger wins out, and dropping her phone, she lunges forward.

Her arms come around my waist, and with a sweep of her foot, she takes my legs from under me, dropping my ass to the ground. I don't have time to admire the move because she straddles me and slams a fist against my jaw.

My first instinct is to restrain her, but when a tear splats against my face, my body goes lax, and I let Jade have her way.

I don't stop her fists, and I take all her anger and sorrow.

Kao is the first to grab hold of Jade, but Noah has to help pull her off of me.

I sit up and don't bother wiping the blood from my busted lip. My eyes never leave Jade as she drops to her knees, with our friends on either side of her. The breath she sucks in sounds painful as if she's choking on the air, then she lets out an agonizing scream.

It's the first time I see just how much she's hurting, and it breaks something inside of me.

Maybe it's the last hope I had of saving our friendship?

The ground might as well tear open and swallow me in a pit of darkness. The finality of losing Jade is too much to bear.

Kao wraps his arms around Jade, and presses her face against his chest, trying his best to console her. His gaze meets mine, and the worry he feels for us makes his blue eyes look like stormy waters.

Noah comes over to me and hands me a piece of toilet paper he must've gotten while I was focused on Jade. I wipe the blood from my mouth and slowly climb to my feet.

"I'm sorry, Jade," I say for the millionth time.

She's the only person I've apologized to in my life.

"I wish I could say I'd do things differently if I had the chance, but there's still no way I'd let you lose your virginity in a guest room at the age of sixteen. You deserved better than that. And you were way too young," I finally get to say the words, standing up for my actions of that fateful night.

Jade shoots forward like a bullet and stops an inch from me. I take in her tearstained cheeks and the broken look in her eyes. "Fuck you, Hunter." She closes the distance between us until I can feel her warm breath on my neck. "Fuck. You."

After twenty months of frustration and with my heart cracked wide fucking open in my chest, I lose my calm and shout, "What the fuck do you want me to say?"

"The truth!" she yells. "What did you do to Brady when you took him home?"

I suck in a deep breath and take a step backward to put some space between us. Struggling to regain my self-control, I growl, "Nothing. I dropped Brady off at home and left."

"Liar," she hisses, and then her face crumbles as she cries, "You're a fucking liar."

Jade storms out of my room, and soon after, the slam of her bedroom door echoes through the suite.

Feeling emotional and fucking exhausted, I sink down on the edge of my bed.

Breathe, Hunter.

Just breathe.

It feels like a tornado swept through me. Fuck, things are worse than I thought. The fact that Jade really thinks I played a part in Brady's suicide sinks in like a ton of bricks.

Hana presses something cold to the cut on my bottom lip. "I'm okay," I mutter.

"I know," she whispers.

Jase, who I thought was missing in action, sits down next to me. Placing his arm around my shoulders, he doesn't say anything. Maybe it's because there are no words for this fucked up situation.

Fallon squeezes my hand before she walks away and slips inside Jade's room with Mila right behind her.

"You should go too," I tell Hana, not wanting her friendship with Jade to be affected by *our* war.

Hana nods and gets up. "Keep the frozen peas against your lip." I take hold of it as Hana leans down, pressing a kiss to my forehead before she leaves.

After a couple of seconds, I drop the peas on the floor.

"Damn," Jase whispers.

"Yeah," I agree.

Noah brings me a tumbler with whiskey, and it makes my lips twitch, but the impending pain has me swallowing my grateful smile. "Thanks."

I gulp a mouthful down, then say, "I didn't know things were that bad."

Jase nods. "Yeah." He lets out a sigh. "Damn."

I turn my face to him. "You're speechless. That's a first." In response to my words, a sad smile forms on his face.

"What are you going to do?" Jase asks the million-dollar question.

I shake my head. "I don't know." I take another sip from the tumbler and let the whiskey burn down my throat. "But I have to do something. She's hurting, and I don't have it in me to take much more."

"It's too much," Noah adds. "It's breaking my fucking heart."

"It's breaking all of us," Jase murmurs.

Thoughts swirl in my head until I grab onto one. "I'm going to let her fight. If she needs to beat me up to feel better, then so be it. Maybe if she has an outlet for her pain, she'll deal with it, and we can become friends again."

Noah pulls an unsure face. "She packs one hell of a punch."

I let out a chuckle. "She sure does. When did she go from playing with dolls to becoming a badass fighter?"

"It's all those summers she spent with Mr. Cole on his ranch," Noah voices. "He's a retired Navy Seal, after all."

"If she fights half as good as him, you're fucked," Jase mumbles under his breath.

"That's no lie. Jade's carrying a lot of pain and anger inside her. This thing won't just blow over," Noah voices something we're all too well aware of after tonight.

I get up and place the empty tumbler on my desk. "I'll just have to suck it up and roll with the punches."

"The shit part is you shouldn't have to," Fallon suddenly says from my open door. "I'm going to get in touch with Brady's family and find out what really happened that night. We all need closure."

45

"Don't," I argue. "If Jade wanted to know the truth, she would've contacted them herself." *Instead of just blaming me.*

Fallon shrugs while letting out a tired sigh. "Well, Jade's calmed down. She said she's going to shower, then crawl into bed."

"Guess I'll do the same," I say, and with that, I walk into my ensuite bathroom.

What a fucking day.

And it's only day one. Still a whole fucking year to go.

Chapter 3

JADE

I stare at my reflection in the mirror after getting dressed for the opening ceremony. It's a longstanding tradition at the academy, so I can't miss it.

My thoughts turn back to last night and regret creeps into my heart. It was a nightmare, to say the least. I thought I'd feel better after hitting Hunter, but I don't. Instead, I feel torn between wanting revenge and feeling guilty.

Why do I feel guilty? Hunter deserved to have his ass handed to him.

Maybe it's because we used to be so close? After all, I did love him for the first sixteen years of my life.

Mostly, I hate that I upset all our friends. Things will have to change. I can't keep hurting the whole group and will have to reign in my temper.

I've never been good at pretending.

I let out a heavy breath.

You'll just have to try to be civil around Hunter and not rip off his head.

My shoulders slump, knowing it's going to be hard to do. I suck in a deep breath before I walk to the door, and opening it, I freeze when I see Hunter's door is open. From where I'm standing, I only have a view of the side of his bed.

You have to try, Jade. For your friends.

I hear movement, and then Hunter walks to his bed and picks up a jacket. I watch him shrug it on, and just like yesterday, I'm struck by how much he's changed.

Sure, I've seen him a couple of times over the past two years, but I always kept my distance and hardly looked at him to avoid a fall out in front of our families and friends.

Before our fight, Hunter seemed indifferent. The few times we argued, I did most of the talking, whereas Hunter just stared at me. He's always come across so indifferent and almost cold. But last night, he lost control of his temper. I've never seen him that angry.

He even shouted at me. He has never raised his voice to me until that moment.

Hunter turns as he buttons his jacket. Even though I hate him with the intensity of a thousand burning suns, I can't help but notice how handsome he's become. He's taller, and his shoulders have become broader. Just like Jase, Kao, and Noah, Hunter has shed the last of his teen body and grown into a man.

His hair is still the same chestnut brown as before, and his eyes sky blue. The contrast has always been striking.

He looks up and stops moving when he sees me. My gaze is drawn to the cut on his bottom lip.

Damn, why does the small imperfection make him look so hot? Life is totally unfair.

When I lost control, it felt good hitting Hunter. But now… I feel like shit warmed over.

He deserved it.

He did.

I keep repeating the words to myself, hoping it will ease the guilt.

We stare at each other for a moment, and as I start to walk down the hallway, Hunter's voice carries to me. "Morning, Jade. The dress looks beautiful on you."

I freeze for a moment, but fisting my hands, I force my feet to move. I do my best to ignore the sadness I heard in Hunter's voice.

"Jade," I hear Jase call behind me. Glancing over my shoulder, I come to a stop so he can catch up to me.

Jase throws his arm around my shoulders and pulls me into his side for a quick hug. He then makes a show of looking at my dress, which is black and nothing spectacular. I've never been one for dresses.

Letting out a low whistle, Jase shakes his head. "Girl, you're looking for trouble."

Frowning, I ask, "Why?"

His facial expression turns all dreamy. "You're looking so hot, I might forget we're just friends and start hitting on you."

His flirty compliment instantly brings a smile to my face, and I let out a soft chuckle.

Before I can respond, Kao appears from the kitchen, holding a mug of steaming coffee. Lord only knows how he can swallow the scalding liquid.

"Nah, it's best the two of you just stay friends. Jase and Jade Reyes won't look good on a wedding invitation," Koa jokes.

Mila walks past us, and mutters, "Jase is a fuck boy. He won't get married even if his life depends on it."

My eyes widen, and I stare at Mila. She glances from Jase to me, and seeing my reaction, she states, "Don't look so shocked, Jade. It's common knowledge Jase is the playboy of the campus."

"Yeah, but you didn't have to be so crass," I say, wondering if I missed a fight between Jase and Mila. "Everyone's cool, right?"

Jase straightens his jacket with a smirk, "You know me. I'm all about peace and love." He starts to walk and passes really close by Mila with a seductive whisper, "There's enough of me for the whole campus. Just say if you want a piece, babe."

My mouth drops open, and I look to Kao for answers. He lets out a chuckle and shakes his head as he turns back to the kitchen to place his empty mug on the counter.

"You're going to wash that, right?" Fallon suddenly asks behind me. Stepping to the side, I see Hana standing beside her with Hunter right behind them.

Kao takes a moment to stare at Fallon, who looks breathtaking in a pale blue dress. "If I leave it on the counter, will you stand there and lay into me for being messy? That way, I can enjoy the view for a couple of minutes longer."

"What the hell did I miss?" I ask no one in particular.

Noah gets up off the couch. I didn't even see him sitting there. "The guys' balls dropped, and the girls noticed. You can all continue flirting and fighting after the ceremony. We're going to be late." He heads for the front door, and as

51

he opens it, his face settles into a bored look. "Oh, look, the kindergartner arrived." He pushes past her and stalks down the hallway.

"Screw you too," Carla, Jase's younger sister, calls after Noah. She lets out a huff, then turns her glare on Jase. "Are you ready? I want to get this day over with."

Damn, I'm confused. Have I been so caught up in myself that I haven't noticed the dynamics of my friends' circle changing?

———————

"Daddy," I call as I break out in a run. Not caring about my image around campus, I fling myself forward as Dad opens his arms wide to catch me. He locks me in a tight embrace before setting me back on my feet. Leaning over to Mom, I give her a hug and kiss her cheek. "Hi, Mom."

"Have you settled in, Bean?" Dad asks while his eyes scan over the other students.

"Yep. I just need to get my class schedule later, then I'm all set for this year."

Dad recognizes someone, and it has me glancing over my shoulder. Kao, Noah, and Mila walk toward us with their families.

A flurry of glitter and colors rushes toward us, then Miss Sebastian grabs hold of Kao, hugging the ever-loving shit out of him before giving me a hug. "How are my god-babies?" She glances around the campus. "Anyone hit on you yet?"

"Hey, Mamma G," I grin, calling her by the special nickname Kao, Noah, Mila, and I have for her, the *G* standing for godmother. "We've all been too busy settling in to be social."

"Speak for yourself," Kao says. "I already snagged a date for the ball."

"Well, at least you're not taking forever like your father did," Miss Sebastian comments.

"I didn't take forever," Uncle Marcus defends himself.

"Honey, it's a wonder my angel-girl, Willow, put up with you for so long. If I didn't have my hands in your chest, I'd seriously doubt there was a heart in there."

I let out a chuckle. Miss Sebastian loves getting Uncle Marcus all riled up.

My gaze lands on Hunter, Jase, Fallon, and Hana, where they're posing, while their mothers take enough photos to fill all the walls of their mansions.

It just solidifies the decision I made to check my temper around Hunter. I don't want to place Fallon and Hana in a position where they'll have to choose between Hunter and me.

Hunter's parents make their way over to us. I notice how Hunter slowly trails behind them, stopping a couple of steps behind them. When he sees that I'm watching him, he takes a step to his right, so Uncle Mason's between us.

Is he hiding behind his father or doing that to keep the peace? Must be the latter. There's no way Hunter's scared of me.

I take a deep breath and smile at Hunter's mom. "It's nice to see you again, Aunty Kingsley."

"You too, hon. Are you excited to start studying?"

"Yeah," I nod, and my smile turns natural. I love Hunter's parents, and just because the two of us don't get along, I shouldn't let it affect my relationship with them.

Aunt Kingsley smiles warmly. "I remember my first day. It was epic. You'll make so many new friends. Just remember to have fun."

"I will."

"It's your final year, Hunter. Are you ready to join CRC Holdings?" I hear my dad ask Hunter.

"Yes. I'll already spend time with my father this year, so it's not too overwhelming when I officially start working."

"As your mom said, don't forget to have fun," Uncle Mason says. "Just nothing that will start a lawsuit. I've had my fill of those."

"God, yes. Please, no lawsuits," Aunt Kingsley adds.

"Did your parents ever tell you about all the trouble they got into while attending here?" Dad asks Hunter.

"Yes," Hunter lets out a burst of laughter. "They always blame Uncle Lake."

"What about me?" Uncle Lake suddenly says as he comes to join us. He looks at Hunter, then asks, "What happened to your lip?"

Oh shit.

I freeze while I wait for Hunter to reply. "The mug nicked it when I had coffee."

I feel torn about the white lie. Part of me is relieved I don't have to explain why I punched him to our families. But the lie only solidifies the fact that it's so easy for Hunter to cover up the truth — just like he did with Brady.

Soon we're one big group, and we begin to move toward the auditorium where the ceremony will be held.

Only the kids of the founding families go to sit on the stage, while their parents join us in the front two rows.

When all the seats are taken, Jase gets up and goes to stand behind the podium. "Welcome to Trinity Academy.

55

As the future chairman of CRC Holdings and Trinity Academy, I am proud to stand here today. Our campus has expanded a great deal, and the dorms were recently renovated. Trinity prides itself on only schooling the best. Past presidents, senators, business magnates, and philanthropists have graduated from Trinity, and we hope to continue with the legacy they have left for us."

When Jase is done talking, his father, Uncle Julian, takes over. The speeches don't last too long, and soon we all file out of the auditorium again. Tables have been set up on the huge lawn between the dorms and the lecture halls. We follow the seating plan, and I pull a face when I see that Hunter's family is situated at the table next to mine.

Can't catch a break from the guy today.

Once we're all seated, servers begin to move between the tables.

Dad orders himself a whiskey, then looks at me, "What would you like, Bean?"

"Just a coke, please."

The server leaves with our order, and Daddy asks, "Did you see the gym on campus?"

"Not yet." I glance in the direction of the gym, that's situated next to the pool house. "I'll probably go check it out this afternoon."

I hope there's a punching bag so I can take all the tension out on it, seeing as I can't hit Hunter.

The morning goes by quickly, and too soon, I walk my parents to their car. "I'm going to miss you."

"You can come home every weekend," Mom says, her voice hopeful.

"I probably will," I admit. "Unless it's exam time."

I kiss and hug both my parents, and as Dad slides in behind the wheel, he says, "If you need anything, just call, and I'll take care of it."

"I know. Love you both."

"Love you most, Bean," Dad says tenderly.

Mom leans over Dad so she can see me. "Love you."

I watch my parents drive off, then begin to walk back to the dorms, but instead of heading to my room, I decide to go see what the gym is like.

The campus is luxurious and modern, with a touch of history. Students pass by me, their eyes focused on their phones. Dressed in only the top brands, I get the impression my fellow students are all competing with each other to look the most fashionable.

I'll definitely end last in that competition. I've never been one to follow the latest fashion trends.

Reaching the gym, high-paced music thumps in the air. Various machines are already occupied, and an aerobics class is just about to start. I search for a punching bag and find a couple hanging at the back of the building.

The beat pulsing around me, and the vibe of energy bouncing off the walls makes me eager to start.

Tomorrow morning first thing I'll be back to beat the ever-loving shit out of the bag.

Grinning and feeling pleased with my discovery, I make my way back to the suite I share with my friends.

Chapter 4

HUNTER

Since my first day at the academy, I've always started my mornings at the gym, and this year will be no different.

I make my way to the upper floor and stepping on a treadmill, I start at a slow jog to warm up. I can still hear the gym's generic music and turn up the volume on my own playlist. Focusing on my breaths, I look down below at the meager amount of students who braved the early hours to get some exercise in before class.

A flash of red draws my attention, and for a moment, I check out the sexy ass swaying across the lower floor.

Damn, the girl looks good in tights.

Then my eyes land on her face, and seeing that it's Jade, the attraction I felt a second ago fizzles a little.

The speed on the treadmill increases, and I have to switch from jogging to running. Jade makes her way over to a row of punching bags, and after putting on a pair of gloves, she begins to lightly bounce around while taking jabs at the bag.

I watch as her blows grow harder and faster. By the time I'm done running and sweat is pouring down my back, I'm not sure if my heart is pounding from the exercise, or from watching Jade beat the shit out of the bag.

I wipe my face and neck before taking a swig from my water bottle, then head down to the ground floor. Jade's so focused that she doesn't see me coming, and it allows me another couple of minutes to watch her.

I'd be a robot not to admit that all sweaty and flushed, Jade looks fucking hot. Glancing around the gym, I notice I'm not the only guy staring at her. One of the juniors stopped training altogether. The weights are forgotten at his feet while he watches Jade with drool practically dripping from his open mouth.

Fucker. He better not get any ideas.

I take a couple of steps forward to catch the junior's gaze, and the moment his eyes focus on me, I shake my head.

All the guys on campus know not to fuck with me. With a light shrug, he resumes his workout.

That's one down.

I turn my attention back to Jade. She's stopped punching, and with her chin raised, her eyes bore into me.

Feeling annoyed that my morning routine has been interrupted, a frown forms on my brow. "Is that seriously what you're going to wear for your workouts?"

A puzzled expression crosses her features then she glances down at the tights and sports bra. "What's wrong with my outfit?"

"It fits like a second skin, Little Bean."

She gives me a skeptical look. "Seriously, Hunter? That's the damn point of exercise clothes, so the fabric doesn't get in the way."

"Yeah, but it… it's too tight. It leaves very little to the imagination." I glance around and scowl at the first guy I catch staring. Flustered, he swings around and rushes to the other side of the building.

You better run, fucker!

Jade shakes her head and lets out an aggravated huff. "Get lost, Chargill." She punches the bag once then glares at me. "Before I forego the bag and lay into you."

That reminds me.

"Great idea. Let's spar."

Jade's body stills, and she looks at me with surprise widening her eyes. "Now you want to fight me? Wasn't the last time enough?"

Raising my eyebrow in a dare, I ask, "I'm offering you the chance to beat me up, and you're asking questions?"

She gestures to the headgear and gloves. "Well, get ready, so I can kick your ass."

After putting on the gear, I hold a head guard out to Jade. "You too. I won't be holding back today."

Jade smirks as she swipes the thing from my hands. "I hope you're ready to have your arrogant, lying ass handed to you."

Stepping onto a mat, I begin to jump lightly. "Give it your best shot, Little Bean."

Jade watches me jump around, and I probably look like an idiot. Let's face it, I'm no professional.

I move forward and jab her shoulder lightly. "Come on. Let's do this before class starts."

Another minute passes, then Jade darts forward. She lands a punch against the side of my head and twisting her body around me, she disappears behind my back. Turning to see where she is, I'm not fast enough and take another blow to the head before she does that thing where she sweeps my legs from under me. Landing hard on my ass,

Jade quickly follows. When she straddles me, I try to throw her off by turning onto my front and pushing myself up on my hands and knees. Jade's like a damn spider monkey, and I can't get her off. Wrapping her arm around my neck in a chokehold, she begins to squeeze. "Tap out."

I shake my head, which only makes her tighten her grip. "Tap out, Chargill. The girls are watching, and it will be disastrous for your dating game if you were to faint like a pussy."

I swear I'm beginning to see stars and giving up for the moment, I reluctantly tap out.

Jade lets go and bouncing to her feet, she gives me a triumphant grin. "You know, for someone who's so damn protective of his friends, you can't fight worth shit."

Climbing to my feet, I grumble, "My grandfather isn't a retired Navy Seal."

"Excuses, excuses," she taunts as she begins to circle me. "You're twice my size. You're stronger, but I still overpower you, *pussy*."

That's the third time she's called me that. Wanting to take her down a peg or two, I dart forward, and with the element of surprise on my side, I pin her arms to her sides and copying the move she's used on me, I take her down.

Once I've straddled her, I restrain her arms down on the mat.

Leaning closer to her, I smirk, "You were saying?"

She squirms under me. "You just had a lucky break. I wasn't paying attention."

"Excuses, excuses," I mock her. Closing the distance between us even more, I can feel her quick breaths fanning my face. "And stop calling me a pussy. It's the last thing you want me thinking of when I'm around you."

She actually looks confused. "Huh?"

"Little Bean," I drop my voice to a low timbre, "You have one, and I have them for breakfast. Let's not go there."

"What. The. Fuck," Jade exclaims while two red spots bloom on her cheeks. "Get off!" Using all her strength, she bucks her hips up, and it only makes me slide forward until my ass is almost over her breasts.

"Damn woman, we're in a public place. I think it would be frowned upon if you were to blow me here."

"I swear to God, Hunter, I'm going to rip your nutsack off and shove it down your throat if you don't get off me right now."

Chuckling, I let go of her and climb back to my feet. "That's one point each. Bring it on, Little Bean."

She attacks me with a rapid succession of punches, finishing with a hard one to my side, which forces the air from my lungs. I let out another breathless chuckle as I try my best to block her quick blows. "You're like a little kitten. Ffttt…ffttt."

Jade stops and gives me a cynical look. "Yeah? Wait until my claws come out. Then you'll have to explain more than just a busted lip to your parents."

"Is that a promise?" I tease, a grin pulling at the corner of my mouth.

"Dude, is that all you can think about?" Jade shakes her head and begins to remove the head guard.

"What?"

She tosses it in a bin so it can be cleaned before the next use. "Sex. Every damn comment you make is somehow related to it."

I follow her and remove the gear. Picking up my towel, I wipe the sweat from my face and the back of my neck. With my eyes on Jade, I take a sip of water, then say, "Seems you bring out that side of me."

Jade grabs her towel and water bottle then begins to walk toward the exit.

"Same time tomorrow?" I call after her.

She doesn't stop walking away from me, but calls out, "Prepare yourself for a world of pain, Chargill."

JADE

I'm still in a flat spin after this morning.

What… ugh… what was that?

I was so caught off guard by Hunter, I even forgot to be angry with him.

Deep in thought, I walk into my room and quickly shower so I can get dressed for class.

When I'm ready and walk to the kitchen to grab a bottle of juice, I find Mila checking her bag.

"Are you prepared for your first day?" I ask.

"Yeah, I just double-checked whether I have enough pens and pencils."

"Girl, I'm pretty sure you have half the stationery department in that bag," I tease her. Mila loves anything stationery related. She has a dozen unused diaries every year just because she thinks the picture on the cover is pretty.

"Are you ready? Then we can walk together," she says as she hoists her bag's strap to her shoulder.

"Sure." I grab my own bag and follow Mila out of the suite. Once we're outside the dorm, I ask, "What's going on with the group?"

"What do you mean?" Mila asks as she glances at a bunch of students passing us by.

"Everyone was either flirting or taking a swing at each other yesterday."

"Oh, that." Mila waves her hand carelessly. "Don't worry about it. It's nothing serious." Then she gives me a questioning look. "Things seem better between you and Hunter. Do I dare hope there won't be a repeat of the fight?"

"Yeah, about that," I pull a regretful face, "I'm sorry you all got dragged into it. I'm not calling a truce, but I'll try to be civil with Hunter, seeing as we have to live in the same suite."

A smile spreads over Mila's face. "It's a start."

Jase walks toward us, and I notice Mila's smile fade.

Yeah, right. Nothing serious, my ass.

"How are my favorite girls this morning?" Jase throws his arm around Mila's shoulder, but she only shakes it off. "Damn, someone's moody.'

67

"Nope, I just don't want you touching me with your slut infested paws," Mila scowls.

Jase throws his hands up with anger flashing across his attractive features. "Fine."

As Jase walks away from us, I turn to my friend. "What the hell, Mila? Where did that come from?"

She lets out a frustrated huff. "A while ago, Jase asked me out on a date, and I said no. He's not the type to commit, and us having a quick fling would only jeopardize our friendship. Since then, he's been seen with a different girl every weekend. Lord only knows what he's doing with them. I don't want him touching me."

My eyes widen as she rambles, and for a moment there's silence before I can find my voice. "Jase asked you out?"

"Yeah." Mila's shoulders slump as she starts to walk again.

I'm pretty sure Mila has the hots for Jase, and the frustration is causing her to act out. I fall in step beside her. "Do you want to date Jase?"

Although she nods, she says, "We can't date. If things go wrong, it will only cause tension in the group, like with you and Hunter."

"Hunter and I never dated. Our situation is different from yours. Besides, how do you know it won't work out?"

Mila rolls her eyes and lets out a heavy breath. "He's a player, Jade. There's no way Jase will ever commit to just one woman."

"You don't know what Jase will do once he falls in love. He might surprise you."

"Yeah, right," she chuckles. We enter the business building and walking into our Strategic Management class, we find seats in the middle of the auditorium. She gives me a reassuring smile, then says, "Don't worry about us. Our little spats are harmless."

"Okay, but I'm here if you need to talk about it." With my thoughts running circles around my two friends, I remove my laptop from my bag and open it up.

Chapter 5

JADE

I haven't been able to focus on my classes because my thoughts have been swamped with the sparring session I had with Hunter this morning.

It was so damn weird and almost like things used to be between us. It only made me realize how much I miss our friendship, but at the same time, I'm filled with guilt. I can't forget about Brady and the part Hunter played in his death.

I'm in two minds about meeting Hunter tomorrow for another sparring session. On the one side, I'll get to beat him up without upsetting our friends. On the other… ugh, I don't know… it feels like I'm betraying Brady in some way.

Letting out a huff, I head over to the restaurant for an early dinner. When I walk inside, I see Fallon and Kao sitting at a table and join them.

"Hey, guys." Taking a seat next to Fallon, I pull a menu closer. "How's your day so far?"

"Good," Fallon answers. "I have to help with the preparations for the welcome ball. You want to help?"

"No, thanks," I chuckle. "There's no way I want to be a part of the decorating committee."

"It's fun," Fallon defends.

"Yeah, but the other girls, not so much. I'll end up punching one of them."

Unfortunately, attending an exclusive academy also means I have to put up with the stuck-up snobs of the world. Some people think just because your daddy's rich, you can walk over people.

"You're way too violent," Kao laughs.

I shrug. "Some people just bring out the bitch in me." Grinning at Kao, I ask, "You said you have a date for the ball? Who is she?"

"Summer Clarke."

Both Fallon and I just stare at Kao until I finally find my words. "Seriously? Why her?"

Summer Clarke and her friends have been our nemeses since we were freshmen in high school. They're the opposite of us – high and mighty, thinking everyone should obey their every whim and order.

"Why not her?" Kao throws a question at me.

"Duh… she's practically the queen bitch."

Kao glances at Fallon, and she gestures to me. "What she said."

"She seemed nice enough to me," Kao states.

"That's because she doesn't consider you a threat to her social standing," Fallon says, then shrugs indifferently. "But, hey, whatever floats your boat."

A waiter approaches our table, and I order a chicken salad. Just then, my phone starts to ring, and seeing that it's Miss Sebastian, a smile forms around my mouth.

"Hey, Mamma G."

Miss Sebastian is my favorite person. She's unique and doesn't care what people think of her. She's all sparkles and always says the funniest stuff to make me laugh.

"My angel-baby! How was your first day?"

"Good. We already got assignments to do."

"I'll call Kao, Noah, and Mila in a minute. I wanted to hear if the four of you would have lunch with me on Saturday?"

"Kao's sitting right here. I can ask him quickly?"

"Great, saves my bedazzled ass the call."

Looking at Kao, I ask, "Mamma G wants to meet us for lunch on Saturday."

"Sure. Just say where."

"He says yes. Where should we meet you?"

"I'll come to Trinity. You can show me around and point out all the chunks of hunks you like."

I let out a chuckle. "There aren't any chunks of hunks, Mamma G. Besides, I'm focusing on my studies and don't have time to date."

She lets out a sigh. "There's always time for a little hanky panky, just not third base. Your daddy will kick my bedazzled ass."

Laughing, I shake my head because there's no way Dad will ever do that. He loves Miss Sebastian way too much, and she gets away with murder, where he's concerned. "Great, we'll see you then."

After ending the call, Kao murmurs, "Trinity is in for a treat and will never be the same again after Miss Sebastian is done with it."

Fallon lets out a burst of laughter. "Yeah." she glances mischievously at me. "We should introduce Summer and her friends to Miss Sebastian."

Laughter explodes from me. "God, that would be priceless."

The rest of the gang walks into the restaurant, and seeing Hunter, my good mood evaporates. As soon as my salad arrives, I spear a piece of chicken with my fork. I'm just about to take the bite when my eyes lock with Hunter's.

A frown instantly forms on my forehead, and I drop the fork on the plate. Shoving my chair back, I mutter, "Lost my appetite."

Before all my good intentions to not fight in front of our friends fly out the window, I quickly leave the restaurant.

I survived yesterday without getting into any fights. Walking into the gym, and seeing Hunter already waiting for me, I remind myself to keep my cool around him.

"Morning, Little Bean," he says way too cheerfully at five in the morning.

And that damn nickname!

I scowl at him and threaten, "Call me little bean one more time."

Hunter grins at me, and I hate that he's so damn attractive you can't help but notice.

I grab a pair of gloves and head guard and try to calm down while putting the gear on.

When we're both ready, and I face Hunter, his grin only widens into a sexy as hell smirk. "Game on, Little Bean."

Asshole.

I dart forward and deliver a couple of punches before bouncing away from him. "Come on, Chargill. You're making this way too easy for me."

He taps me lightly on my shoulder, which has my eyes rolling. "Stop playing around," I grind the words out.

Hunter shoots forward and wrapping an arm around my waist, he tries to sweep my feet from under me, but I'm prepared and acting fast, I reverse the move on him, dropping him to the ground.

He lets out a bark of laughter and climbs back to his feet. "How was your first day of classes?"

The question catches me off guard, and for a moment, I blink at him until I realize he's trying to make small talk. "We're only here to spar, Chargill. Don't pretend to be interested in my life."

Tilting his head to the side, a serious look tightens his features. "What makes you think I'm pretending?"

I shrug even though anger bubbles to the surface. "You couldn't have cared less two years ago, so now shouldn't matter as well." Done with this sparring session, I strip off the gear.

Grabbing my towel and water bottle, I walk away, so I don't do something that will attract everyone in the gym's attention.

Before I can reach the exit, Hunter catches up to me, and the moment we're outside the building, he grabs hold of my hand and drags me off to the side. "I didn't care?" he bites the question out. "It's because I fucking cared that I stopped you."

Raising my chin, I cross my arms over my chest and meet his glare with my own heated one. "You could've fooled me. My relationship with Brady had nothing to do with you. You shouldn't have stuck your nose in my business and –"

"There was no way in hell I was going to let you have sex at sixteen!" he practically barks at me.

"My almost having sex is not the problem," I bite out. "What happened when you took Brady home?"

I just want the truth. I want to know what Hunter did to Brady.

I need to know.

Hunter takes a step closer, and I have to lift my chin higher to keep eye contact. He clenches his jaw, and anger ripples off him in waves, clashing against my own.

"How many times do I have to say it?" he growls. "I didn't do anything to Brady. I dropped him off and went home."

"Liar," I hiss. My emotions become an overwhelming whirlpool of anger and hurt.

Hunter glares at me for a moment, and I can see the emotions warring on his face as he struggles to reign in his own anger. Slowly a defeated look shadows his features, and then he throws his hands in the air. "God knows I've tried, but no more. We're done."

As he starts to walk away from me, I yell, "We're not done until I get my revenge."

Not even looking back, he growls, "Whatever, Daniels."

It takes a moment to realize Hunter didn't call me Jade, or bean, or little bean.

Just Daniels.

Uncertainty creeps into my mind, but I'm too angry to pay it any attention and mutter, "Right. Whatever, Chargill."

Chapter 6

HUNTER

It's only been three days since we started classes, and I'm ready for this year to be over.

Making my way to the restaurant for dinner, my irritation grows with every damn girl that tries to get my attention. It usually wouldn't bother me, but today I have zero patience left for the female species after my fight with Jade.

"Hunter!" My jaw clenches at the sound of Jessica Atwood's overly sweet voice.

Not slowing down, I hear Jessica's heels slapping against the cobbled stone path as she tries to catch up with me. Grabbing hold of my arm, she darts in front of me.

Coming to a stop, I give her an aggravated look.

She doesn't let go of my arm as she flips her hair back while a pretentious smile forms on her face. "Have dinner with me."

I suck in a deep breath, so I don't shrug her off with a curse. Instead, I pull my arm free and move to walk around her while bluntly uttering, "No."

Not getting the message, Jessica falls into step next to me. "You need to eat, don't you?"

"Not with you," I mutter.

Taking hold of my arm for a second time, she tries to pull me to a stop again, but I yank away from her and give her a dark glare. "Fucking stop already. I'm not interested in you, woman."

Hurt flashes across her perfect features.

Too perfect.

When everything around you is perfect, you gain an appreciation for flawed things because it adds balance to your life.

"You don't have to be so mean, Hunter," she chastises while quickly glancing around to see if anyone else heard what I said to her.

I've dealt with her kind enough to know if you give them an inch, there's no getting rid of them. Also, Mom would slap me into a new damn blood group if I ever get involved with the likes of Jessica.

Knowing I have to be as fucking clear as daylight with this woman, I lock eyes with her. "I'm not a social ladder. Find another guy to help you get to the top because it sure as hell won't be me." I turn to continue walking, then pause. "Another thing, don't ever touch me again or pretend we move in the same circle."

Done with her, I stalk to the damn restaurant even though I don't have any appetite.

Doing my best to ignore the wave of whispers my presence causes as I enter the establishment, I make my way to our reserved tables and sit down next to Jase, who's already busy scarfing down a pizza.

"You sure you're not related to Uncle Lake?" I ask. Uncle Lake and Jase will eat anyone under the table.

Jase just smirks at me then asks, "Why do you look like you're about to kill someone?"

"Fucking women," I grumble.

A waiter appears next to me, and I order a whiskey.

"No food?" Jase asks when the waiter leaves.

I reach over and grab a slice of pizza just so he'll shut up.

"Good boy," the fucker croons.

I glare at him. "You tired of living?"

Jase lets out a chuckle while picking up another slice, and I watch him obliterate it in seconds before he says, "You love me too much to kill me."

"Don't push your luck," I warn, and then unable to keep my face stoic any longer, a grin pulls at my lips. Even though we banter a lot about killing each other, Jase knows I'd die for him.

Kao and Noah join us just as the waiter brings my drink.

"I'll have one of those," Noah orders, then he lets out a sigh.

"Shit day?" I ask before I take a sip from the tumbler.

"You have no idea," Noah mutters. He looks at me for a couple of seconds then says, "We need to have all the freshmen go to an induction course on stay the fuck away from Noah, Kao, Hunter, and Jase."

"Hey," Jase jumps in. "Leave me out of your cock-blocking mission."

"Don't you get tired of the girls?" Noah asks while shaking his head.

Jase grins, "I have the stamina of a thoroughbred stallion."

I let out a bark of laughter. "Stallion, my ass."

Kao looks over a menu while asking, "Does that mean the lot of you aren't taking dates to the ball?"

Just thinking of the ball, I pull a disgusted face.

Jase picks up a napkin and wipes his mouth. "I'm going with Mila."

Kao lets out a burst of amused laughter. "Does Mila know this?"

"Do I know what?" Mila suddenly asks.

My head snaps up, and seeing that Jade is with the girls, I glare at the tumbler of whiskey in front of me, so I don't have to acknowledge her presence as she takes a seat across from me.

"You're going to the ball with me," Jase states as if Mila has no choice in the matter.

"Like hell," Mila grumbles.

Jase glances around the table. "Do any of you have dates, besides Kao?"

"Nope," Fallon lets the word pop from her lips.

Hana and Jade shake their heads where Noah and I just stare at Jase.

Jase grins at Mila. "That means we're going in a group, aka you're going with me."

Mila gives Jase a disgruntled look before she picks up a menu.

When the waiter comes to take the new orders, I stare at the amber liquid in front of me, contemplating whether I should leave.

Feeling eyes on me, my gaze lifts until they collide with Jade's brown ones.

Not breaking eye contact, I finish what's left of my whiskey, then get up. "You coming?" I ask Jase as I begin to turn away from the table.

"Don't leave on my account," Jade says, her tone daring me to stay.

A hundred comebacks race through my mind, but every one of them will only show Jade that I care. Instead, I give her a cold look before leaving the restaurant.

Jase quickly follows behind me. "Things still bad between you and Jade?"

I let out a huff of air. "Bad is the understatement of the fucking year. I'm done trying with her."

We walk in silence for a minute, then Jase asks, "Really? How are you going to handle being around her then?"

"Like I handle any other girl."

With zero patience and a shitload of disdain.

"Ouch." Jase gives me a worried look. "You don't think that's overkill? We're talking about Jade. She's one of us."

"She decided our friendship was over long before I did. Why should I treat her as one of us, when she clearly doesn't give a fuck about me?"

"Shit." Jase throws his arm around my shoulders. "I'm sorry it came to this. I was hoping you and Jade would be able to deal with the past once you were living under the same roof."

"So much for hoping, right?"

"Yeah, right."

When we get to the suite, I go to shower and not in the mood to run into Jade again, I decide to work on one of my assignments until I'm tired enough to sleep.

A couple of hours later, I yawn as I close my laptop. I tuck it back in my bag for tomorrow's class then crawl under the covers. I'm just about to switch off the light when my door opens, and Fallon and Hana come creeping into my room with their pillows tucked under their arms.

"Hey," I whisper as I scoot to the middle of the bed to make space for the girls.

Fallon climbs in on my right and Hana on my left, and then they snuggle up to my sides.

"Jade told us you had another fight," Fallon whispers as she reaches over to the lamp, turning it off.

"Yeah."

"Are you okay?" Hana asks softly.

I don't know why the girls bother bringing pillows when they always end up using my arms to sleep on anyway.

"I'll be okay," I answer Hana.

"Love you, Hunter," Fallon whispers sleepily.

"In this life and the next," Hana adds.

"Love you, too."

I lie awake as the girls drift off to sleep. Having them with me always helps. Ever since we were little, we used to sleep in the same bed whenever our families got together for a visit or going away on vacations. Our families share a bond that most blood-related relatives don't even have – loyalty, undying love, and a fierce protectiveness toward each other.

Even though they're asleep, I still whisper, "Thanks for always being there for me when I need you most."

JADE

Being up at the crack of dawn, I open my door, so I can go get some coffee. When Hunter's door slowly creeks open, I freeze but seeing Fallon and Hana sneak out, I grin at them.

Walking to the kitchen, I ask, "You want some coffee?"

"Oh God, please," Fallon mumbles, still half asleep.

"Why did I agree to help with the preparations for the ball?" Hana complains, her eyes hardly open.

"Cause you love me."

I chuckle at their conversation while I begin to make our coffees. I know Fallon and Hana are really close with Hunter, and if they were forced to choose between him and me, they'd rush to his side in a heartbeat. It's just the way things work in our circle. Even though Noah and Kao are friends with Hunter, they'd choose me.

And that's why I haven't lost my shit with Hunter. He's been super cold toward me since our fight, but I won't let it get to me.

I carry the mugs over to the living room and sit down on the couch with my own. After taking a sip, I ask, "How are the preparations going? The ball's only in three weeks. Why do you have to get up so early?"

"Because it's the only time the committee can meet. This year they want to go with a theme." Fallon pulls a face that has me chuckling.

"Black and white is so overdone," Hana complains.

"Yeah, and masked balls," Fallon adds.

"Every theme has been done to death," I mutter before bringing my mug to my lips. I swallow the warm liquid down, then grin. "You could go with bitches and playboys. That would fit right in on campus."

Fallon snorts. "Can you imagine the committee's reaction if I propose that?"

"It would be hilarious."

After a minute of silence, Fallon says, "What about rainbows? My dad always calls my mom his rainbow, and I love it. If we make that the theme, we can at least wear any color we want to."

I get up and smile at Fallon. "I love the idea."

Hana looks excited as she agrees, "Yeah, we just need to convince the other girls."

A slight frown forms on my forehead. "Fallon, you're the heir to the Reyes group. You don't need to convince anyone of anything."

She scrunches her nose. "I hate using my family name to get my way."

When her coffee is finished, I reach over and take her mug. "Yeah, but at the end of the day, you represent your family. Don't let people walk over you."

She thinks over my words, then agrees, "You're right. I'll just tell them we're going with a rainbow theme."

"Thank God," Hana sighs. "That will save us from having to listen to them argue for an hour."

Chuckling, I go rinse the mugs so I can get to the gym.

I'm just about to leave the suite when Hunter comes out of his room. He's dressed in a pair of shorts and a vest. I dislike shorts but on Hunter... damn him for being so hot.

Scowling at myself, I stare at Hunter while trying to figure out why I find him so attractive compared to the other guys. Yeah, I know my friends are good-looking, but with Hunter, it's different.

Your heart's beating faster because he infuriates you so much.

He catches me staring at him, and tilting his head to the left, he says, "Wow, that's a nice shade of bitch you're wearing today."

Deciding not to ruin everyone's day with another fight, I bite my tongue and roll my eyes at him. "Not today, Satan. Not today."

Knowing that Hunter will be going to the gym, I follow the path to the woods behind the campus, and I fall into a steady pace as I jog.

I wonder how long Hunter is going to keep lying about what happened that night. With the trees and shrubbery swallowing me, my thoughts turn to the last time I saw Brady.

Two Years Ago…

My heart pounds a mile a minute as I stare at my reflection in the mirror.

Wearing my favorite summer dress, I've taken extra care with my appearance. I've even foregone my usual boots for a pair of sandals.

Tonight is the night.

The thought makes my heartbeat speed up until it feels like it might jump right out of my chest.

Brady and I have been best friends since our first day of school, but things changed a year ago when we turned fifteen. I can't believe we've been dating for a year already.

Brady was my first kiss… my first and only love. We've talked about having sex for a while now, and I'm ready to take the next step with him.

But first, we have to go to Jase's birthday party.

Picking up the present I got for Jase, I leave my room. When I take the stairs down, I hear Dad laughing, but the moment I walk into the living room, the smile drops from his face.

His brows furrow. "Why are you wearing a dress?"

I roll my eyes and let out a sigh. "'Cause it's normal for girls to wear dresses, Daddy."

I notice how Mom tries to hide a smile by covering her mouth with her hand, but my cousins, Ryker and Mila, don't even bother as they grin because Dad's being his usual overprotective self.

"Yeah, but it shows your legs," Dad grumbles, and it has Ryker chuckling. Dad gives him a dark scowl, "Does Logan let Mila go out looking like that?"

Ryker shrugs. "My father doesn't have much of a choice in what Mila wears, because whatever Mom says goes in our household."

Dad shakes his head, then looks at Mom. "Are you okay with Jade wearing that dress?"

Mom clears her throat and smiles at me. "I think Jade looks beautiful."

It only makes the look on Dad's face darken. "I'm not going to win, am I?"

I shake my head and walking to the chair he's sitting on, I place my hand on his shoulder and press a kiss to his cheek. "Daddy, just tell me I look pretty. It's not like I'm going to a club. I'll be with the group at Jase's house, so you have nothing to worry about."

My group of friends consists of my cousins and family friends. We're a tight-knit group of sixteen kids who grew up together.

Dad lets out a hopeless sigh. "As long as you and Brady don't go sneaking off."

Sometimes Dad's sixth sense is scary.

"Daddy," I begin to worry I somehow gave away that I plan on losing my virginity tonight. I hope none of my emotions show on my face as I say, "You know Brady is sweet and caring."

Dad locks eyes with me, his expression saying he doesn't care much for what I think of Brady. "He's a boy, and you're a girl. No amount of being sweet and caring can overrule hormones."

My eyes widen, and I glance at Ryker and Mila, who look like they're seconds away from cracking up, then I turn my shocked expression back to dad. "Are you seriously going to give me the birds and the bees talk in front of everyone?"

"That's enough, Rhett," Mom scolds Dad. She gets up and comes to give me a hug. "Have fun, Bean."

Playfully, I narrow my eyes at Mom because she still calls me by the nickname they gave me as a baby.

With a loving smile, she murmurs, "You'll always be our little bean." Then she turns to Ryker. "Drive safely and no drinking."

"Yes, Aunty Evie."

I lean down and give Dad a hug. "Love you, Daddy."

His arms wrap around me, and he pulls me down until I'm sitting on his knee. Giving me a worried look, he says, "I worry about you, Bean. Boys only have one thing on their minds."

"Rhett, I'm certain Brady's mind doesn't work anything like yours did when you were a teenager."

Mom gives him a stern glare, which has Dad looking chastised. "If I knew I'd be paying for my sins…"

"What? You'd walk the straight and narrow? We both know that's impossible when it comes to Rhett Daniels and his friends."

"Mhh…" I tease. "I feel like there's an interesting story I want to hear."

Dad pushes me up. "Nope, nothing interesting in my past." He rises from the chair and walks toward the front door. "Have fun, guys. Ryker, have Jade home by midnight."

I grin, and when I reach the front door, I press another kiss to Dad's cheek.

He gives me a warm smile and whispers, "Love you, Bean."

The drive to the Reyes' Mansion is a quick one, and when I walk out onto the veranda, Hunter calls out, "Bean's finally here."

Grinning at him, I break out into a run. Hunter catches me in a big bear hug, and asks, "How's my favorite girl?"

"Good." He waits for me to press a kiss to his cheek before setting me down on my feet. Glancing over his designer jeans and t-shirt, I say, "I like the new clothes. You always look good in black."

"Because it fits my dark soul," he teases.

"Yeah, right." Turning to Jase, I say, "Happy birthday, Jase. How does it feel to be twenty?"

"No different from yesterday." Jase gives me a warm smile. "I still can't legally drink, which sucks huge hairy donkey balls."

I scrunch my nose. "Eww."

As I step closer to Kao, he gets up and gives me a hug. "Hey, Little Bean."

Smiling, I hug him back. Every day, I thank my lucky stars that I have such a big group of friends. Our parents are either related, best friends, or business partners.

"When are you going to stop calling me Little Bean?" I ask Kao.

Frowning at me, he asks, "So, it's okay if Hunter calls you Little Bean, but not me?"

Shaking my head, I step forward and wrap my arms around his waist. Resting my cheek against his chest, I mumble, "He calls me Bean. Lose the little, and I'll stop giving you lip."

Pressing a kiss to the top of my head, Kao replies, "You'll always be Little Bean to me."

"Jade!" Mila calls from the sliding doors. "Brady's here."

"Can you send him out here?" I'm about to walk to the veranda, but Hunter grabs hold of my hand and glares down at me.

"How's Brady treating you? You're not doing anything stupid, right?"

My eyes widen at his words. "Gross, Hunter. You sound like my dad."

"Unlike your dad, I'll fuck Brady up if he tries anything with you."

Shaking my head, I hold Hunter's intimidating gaze. "Yeah, you and every other man in my life. Give it a rest already."

The blue of his eyes darkens around the pupil, which is a clear sign he's dead serious. Not wanting him to give Brady a hard time, I close the distance between us and take hold of his jacket. Giving him a pleading look, I say, "Let it go, please. I won't do anything irresponsible."

Hunter tilts his head to the left, his features not softening at all as he stares at me.

Damn, he's just like his father.

"Trust me, Hunter," I whisper.

He lets out a deep breath, then says, "I trust you, but I'm still going to kick his ass if he tries anything."

Forest, Fallon's younger brother, comes to stand by us and pats Hunter's shoulder. Even though he's a year younger than me, the older boys in our group never treat him like a kid. Nope, they keep the special kiddie treatment for the girls.

"Dude, chill. Brady's the shy wimpy kind. Jade could knock him out with one punch."

"Forest!" I chastise him. "You don't have to be mean. Brady's just sensitive. Unlike the lot of you."

Deciding I've had enough lectures for one day, I go to greet the rest of my friends, and when I'm done, I turn to the most important people in the group.

My girls.

Smiling, I walk to where Mila, Fallon, and Hana are standing with Brady.

When I reach them, I hook my arm through Brady's and grin at my friends. "Thank you for keeping Brady company while I did my rounds."

"Shouldn't I greet everyone?" Brady asks, his eyes scanning over my group of friends. Brady, being an introvert, is always anxious around my friends.

"No, it's okay." I glance up at him, and when we make eye contact, my stomach flips, and the sensation makes my heart beat faster. "Do you want anything to drink?"

"No, thanks. I'm good."

More people begin to arrive, and soon music is blasting as the party gains momentum. Uncle Julian and Aunt Jamie, Jase's parents, have gone out for dinner and will be back in a couple of hours. Knowing my time is limited, I glance up at the mansion. The house has eight bedrooms, and I intend to borrow one of them tonight. I know the east wing is quiet and that Jase's parents only use that part of the house for guests. It's also the furthest point from the party.

My girls said they'd cover for me if anyone asks where I am.

Turning my eyes away from the house, I look at my friends. Mila leans closer to me and whispers, "Are you sure?"

I nod and give her a reassuring smile. "Never been more sure in my life."

When I first mentioned to the girls that I want to lose my virginity to Brady, they all protested. They thought I wanted to have sex because girls in our grade were losing their virginities like it was nobody's business. But after I told them how much I love Brady, they supported me.

I take hold of Brady's hand. "Do you want to take a walk with me?"

Brady grins and links our fingers together. "Yeah, sure."

We walk back into the house, and I head in the direction of the stairs. Peeking over my shoulder, I make sure no one noticed we left the party before we take the stairs up.

"This place is huge," Brady comments as we stop so he can peek into the rooms and satisfy his curiosity.

"Yeah. The east wing is quieter, though. Aunty Jamie only uses it for guests."

Brady's always been the silent and introverted type, so I know it's up to me to start the conversation.

When the music has faded to nothing more than a thumping beat in the distance, I glance up at Brady. "I wanted to talk to you about something."

"Yeah? What?" Brady turns his warm brown eyes to me. I first fell in love with his soft, kind eyes. Brady's the kind of person who wouldn't hurt a fly.

"We've been dating for a year, and I was wondering whether you're ready to take the next step in our relationship?"

A nervous look tightens his boyish features, and I almost begin to regret asking when he swallows hard and then says, "First, I need to tell you something."

A wide smile spreads across my face. "Okay, let's go into the room so we can have privacy."

I shut the door behind us, and I'm about to reach for the switch against the wall to turn on the light, but Brady's hand darts out, stopping me. "Can... can we leave the light off?"

It's not that dark with the curtains open, and knowing how painfully self-conscious he is, I agree. "Sure." There's a minute's silence, then I ask, "Do you want to sit on the bed while we talk?"

Brady nods his head, and when we're both sitting, he takes hold of my hand. His eyes shine as they slowly meet mine. "I want my first time to be with you, as well. I don't know what I did to deserve you, Jade."

My smile softens and I press a kiss to his mouth. "I love you, Brady."

"I love you too, Jade." A nervous expression flits across Brady's face. Patiently I wait for him to continue with whatever he wanted to talk about.

He takes a deep breath and rising back to his feet, he nervously grips hold of the hem of his shirt. "It's hard to talk about it."

Thinking that he's referring to us having sex, I give him a warm smile to encourage him.

Before Brady can say anything else, the door to the room slams open and bright light blinds me for a moment.

"What the fuck is going on in here?" Hunter's voice is like a bolt of lightning.

My eyes dart to the doorway, and seeing Hunter with our friends right behind him, embarrassment washes over me like hot lava.

"N-n-nothing," Brady stammers, his eyes wider than mine.

"Nothing, my ass," Hunter barks. "Get away from her."

Cowering, Brady rushes to the door without even looking at me.

"Hunter!" I jump off the bed and come to a stop right in front of him. "You're overreacting."

His eyes blaze down on me. "I'm pretty sure I'm not. Any idiot can guess what the two of you were doing up here in the dark."

My cheeks are on fire and needing to make sure Brady is okay before I get into a fight with Hunter, I try to leave the room. Hunter grabs my arm, pulling me back. "You stay here. I'll take Brady home."

Not waiting to hear what I think or how I feel, Hunter leaves and rushes after Brady.

Shocked by how quickly the night turned into a disaster, my eyes dart over my friends.

Mila is the first to react and comes to place her arm around me. "Hunter noticed the instant you and Brady left," she explains.

"He ruined it all," I mutter, my embarrassment bleeding into disappointment.

Chapter 7

HUNTER

Things have been quiet with Jade, which I should be thankful for, but it grates me that even though we live in the same suite, we never talk.

Thinking of the devil…

I'm on my way to the library when I spot Jade coming out of the wide doors. Her attention is on a book in her hands, and it gives me a moment to steel myself before I have to interact with her.

"Hunter." Hearing Melinda Roberts' voice, I let out a groan.

I glance over my shoulder and seeing that she's with her group of friends, which includes Jessica Atwood, my mood instantly sours.

Fuck, I'm not in the mood for this.

When Melinda reaches me, she tries to give me an intimidating scowl. "Jessica told me how nasty you were to her."

I let out an aggravated breath and turning away from the group of socialites, I come face to face with Jade. Her dark eyes flick from me to the group behind me.

"Don't turn your back on me," Melinda almost screeches.

Right now, I'd rather face a hundred Jades before I have to spend a second with Melinda and her clique.

A frown begins to form on Jade's forehead, and she comes to stand next to me, facing the girls. "Who the hell do you think you're talking to?"

Her words shock me, and slowly I turn my head so I can see her face.

Fuck, she looks pissed, but I'm not missing this for anything in the world.

I watch Melinda's cheeks redden with outrage. "This is none of your business."

Jade lets out a dark chuckle, and I wonder whether I should warn the girls their lives might be in danger.

"Oh, honey." Jade smiles sympathetically at Melinda. "What you fail to realize is that Hunter Chargill is none of your business. Stop aiming so high. The fall back to earth might kill you."

Melinda sneers at Jade. "What *you* fail to realize is that we have the same status. You don't get to talk down to me."

Jade takes a threatening step closer to the girls. "That might be so, but it won't stop me from kicking your ass."

Melinda flicks her hair over her shoulder and gives me an angry look. "We're not done, Hunter. We'll talk when your dog is on a leash."

"Fuck," I exclaim as Jade drops her book and pulls her arm back. I move fast and wrapping my arms around Jade, I yank her back before she can hit Melinda.

"Let go of me," Jade hisses.

"Nope, it's too early in the year for lawsuits." I tighten my hold on her, pinning her back to my chest. My icy glare collides with Melinda's. "You better leave if you don't want your face rearranged."

Luckily the girls turn around, and in a cloud of disapproving remarks, they leave.

Jade stops struggling, and I peek at her face to make sure it's safe to let her go.

She gives me an annoyed look. "I wasn't going to hit her hard."

"Yeah, right." Stepping away from her, I tilt my head. "Since when do you care about how people address me?"

Rolling her eyes, she crouches down and picks up her book. "It's not about you. If the students get away with treating you like shit, they'll do the same to Fallon and Hana."

I never thought of that. "And here I was trying to fly under the radar."

Jade lets out a burst of air. "Yeah, that's never going to happen. Grow a pair and stand up for yourself. I don't want my friends to suffer, because you're a coward."

I have to close my eyes and grind down on my teeth, so I don't lose my shit. "You know, for someone that's so fucking vocal about people staying out of her business, you're damn quick to stick your nose into others." Not giving her time to respond, I stalk away.

That woman will be the end of my sanity one of these days!

Before I reach the steps of the library, Nate Sparks, a junior at the academy, approaches me. His friends are right behind him when he says, "You should give Melinda a chance. She's a sweet piece of ass."

After my fall out with Jade, I have zero patience left. "Fuck off."

"You seriously need to get laid, dude," Nate chuckles.

Stepping closer, I crowd his personal space. "Who the fuck do you think you're calling dude?"

Cowering backward, he holds his hands up in a surrendering gesture. "Chill. I'm just being friendly."

Pushing past the fucker, I growl, "We're not friends."

I stalk into the library, and students quickly part in front of me.

It's going to be a long fucking year.

Just wanting to hang with my friends, I agree when Jase says we should all go to *Studio 9*, a club nearby that only the elite can get into.

I'm dressed in a black pair of chinos and a button-up shirt. Grabbing my wool-cashmere topcoat, I shrug it on. When I step into the living room, Mila lets out a whistle and teases, "Ladies, hold onto your ovaries. All the hotness in the world just arrived."

"Yeah, and dressed in black just like his soul," Jase adds, shooting Mila a scowl.

When will my friend admit he is hopelessly in love with Mila?

"Everyone ready?" I ask as I adjust the Rolex on my wrist.

"We're waiting for Jade. Fallon is trying to get her into a dress," Hana explains.

"Fallon failed," Jade suddenly says behind me. I glance over my shoulder, and my eyes land on the ample cleavage showing from the low-cut silk blouse she's wearing.

I press my lips together, trying not to comment about what I think of her clothes, but fail miserably. "I don't know why you make a fuss about wearing a dress when your top hardly covers everything."

"Someone wants to die young," she mutters as she walks by me.

JADE

Asshole.

When we step out of the building, Jase grabs Mila's hand and drags her to his car. When she smacks him against the shoulder, I grin, but it quickly drops from my face when I notice Fallon and Hana following after Kao and Noah.

"Hana," I call out and jog to catch up with her. "Will you go with Jase and Mila?" I really don't want to be in the same car as Hunter.

"Sure." She walks over to Hunter and links her arm with his.

I climb in the back, and when Noah gets in next to me, I grin at Fallon. She scrunches her nose at me as she takes the passenger seat, next to Kao.

Yep, love is in the air. It's only a matter of time before they pair up.

Now that I'm spending more time with my friends, I'm actually getting excited as I watch them fight their feelings for each other.

The drive to the exclusive club is filled with small talk. The parking area is already full when we arrive, which is typical for a Friday night.

Due to the Reyes, Chargill, and Cutler names being practically godlike, we're seating in the VIP section that overlooks the entire bottom floor.

Jase goes to stand by the chrome barrier and glances over all the girls' below, probably looking for his next target.

A waiter takes our drinks order, and I settle for a coke. I swing my leg lightly, trying to get into a party mood.

"Let's go dance. We'll loosen up faster that way," Fallon says, already getting up and heading for the stairs. Mila, Hana, and I follow behind her, and she quickly makes space for us on the crowded floor.

I sway to the beat as I smile at my friends, but it's not even a full minute, and a group of guys joins us. Justin, Nate, Chris, and Eric are basically the male equivalents of Summer Clarke and her friends.

"Hey, Fallon. You're looking good," Justin addresses her.

"Justin." Her tone is tolerant at best, which means my friend doesn't like the guy at all.

"Mind if we join you?" he asks, his eyes roving over us before they stop on Mila.

My right eyebrow darts up in warning because I won't let anyone mess with my cousin, and it has me answering, "We don't need the company."

Nate saunters closer to me, a smirk pulling at his mouth. "Don't be a bitch about it. We're all here to have fun."

"This is her being nice, Sparks," Hunter suddenly talks behind me. "You better go before she gets violent."

Glancing over my shoulder, I scowl at Hunter, but before I can let him have a piece of my mind, my cousin Ryker and his best friend Tristan head toward us.

I haven't seen Tristan in a while, and go to hug him. "Hey, stranger. How are you?"

Smiling, he hugs me back. "Good. How's the academy?"

With a disgruntled look, I reply, "Probably still the same as when you attended."

Tristan is five years older than me and has already been working for two years. Lucky him.

"It's not all bad." Tristan moves to greet Mila and Fallon, and when he gets to Hana, his smile warms, and he hugs her a little bit longer.

Come on, Jade. You're just seeing things. Not all your friends have the hots for each other.

When Tristan keeps his arm around Hana's waist, both my eyebrows pop up. He only has to stare at Justin and Nate, and they retreat into the crowd.

Yeah, no one would dare screw with Carter Hayes' youngest son. It's the same as trying to take on Hunter or Jase. And it's definitely not my imagination. Something is going on between Tristan and Hana.

Leaning closer to Ryker, I ask, "Does Tristan like Hana?"

My cousin nods. "Hana keeps playing it down, but I think she's starting to warm up to the idea."

Wide-eyed, I stare at Ryker. "When did this happen?"

"At the Christmas gathering. You were at the ranch."

"Oh." My gaze turns back to Hana and Tristan, and I comment, "They're complete opposites. Tristan is just like his father, all sharp edges where Hana is soft and quiet like her mom. Do you think they could work as a couple?"

"Anything is possible," Ryker replies, then he frowns at me. "Why are we standing on the dance floor. Let's go upstairs."

I leave my friends to dance with Tristan and Hunter and follow Ryker to our table where Kao and Noah are enjoying their drinks. Jase has probably already found his next lay.

Once we're seated, I glance around the room, then ask, "Aren't there any girls here you like?"

Ryker doesn't even look around and just shakes his head. Grinning at me, he says, "I'd rather spend time with you."

A waiter interrupts us to take Ryker's order.

I glance down to the dance floor and see that only Tristan and Hana are left dancing.

Soon the conversation around the table is flowing smoothly, and I'm lulled into a relaxed state.

Who would've thought Hunter and I could be civil for so long. Not that we're talking to each other, but hey, I guess miracles do happen.

Chapter 8

HUNTER

After spending the last hour being Jase's wingman, I'm ready to call it a night.

Jase is talking to a brunette, and I'm stuck with her friend. I'm pretty sure her hair is gray, and I keep wondering why someone would willingly do that to their hair. My mom's been dyeing the ever-loving shit out of her own in her fight against gray strands.

"So, you attend Trinity Academy?" the girl asks for the tenth time.

I just nod in response. At this rate, I might die of boredom.

"That must be so cool."

I'm busy zoning out and totally caught off guard when another girl snuggles up to my side, linking her arm with mine in a possessive way. My eyes dart to her face, and then shock ripples over me.

What the hell?

Jade smiles lovingly up at me, and it has me doing another double-take.

"Did you drink?" It's the only reason I can think of for her weird behavior.

"Just a little. I stole the last of Ryker's whiskey when he wasn't looking. Did you miss me, baby?" Jade takes hold of my arm and positions it around her.

Baby?

What. The. Actual. Fuck?

Jade doesn't let my shocked silence hinder her and snuggles even closer to me, and it makes her cleavage look double the size where it's pressed against my side.

When she stretches her body and presses a kiss to my jaw, I swear it feels like my mind is malfunctioning because all I can do is blink while staring at her.

Then Jade turns her head to the girl I was talking to and sneers, "I don't appreciate it when girls drool over my man. Get lost."

I begin to frown, still at a total loss when it comes to finding the right words for this fucking weird moment.

The girl leaves with an offended look on her face, and when she's out of hearing distance, Jade gives me a grin that's nothing short of evil. "Payback's a bitch, Chargill. If

I don't get to be happy, then you don't. How does it feel to be cock blocked?"

Jade pulls away, and all I can do is stare at her ass as it sways its way back to our group's table. I don't know whether I should be impressed she can act so well, or to be pissed because she's decided to play games with me.

Tapping Jase on the shoulder, I gesture toward our table. "Let's go get a drink."

Jase gets the girl's phone number, and as we make our way back to the VIP section, my eyes are glued to Jade.

If I'm honest with myself, even though I was shocked out of my mind by what she did, I can't deny the fact that she stirred something in me I haven't felt before around another woman. It's fucking confusing.

Jase and I take the only two open seats left, and it situates me across from Jade. We place our order for drinks, and while I wait, I keep staring at Jade. She's either oblivious or making a show of not giving a fuck that my eyes are on her.

Jase suddenly jumps up, almost giving me a heart attack as he yells, "We have to try this game!"

If only my friend knew how tired I was of games.

"What game?" Tristan asks. I'm surprised he managed to take his attention off Hana long enough to ask. It's clear the guy is head over heels for her. Then again, with Hana being half Korean, she has an exotic beauty you can't help but notice.

"The arrow spins and whoever it lands on has to do the dare the app gives."

"I'm bored out of my mind, so we might as well give it a try," Noah approves.

Jase places the phone in the middle of the table and presses the spin button. We watch the arrow turn, and it lands on Mila.

Hug the person you like the least.

Mila grins as she gets up and walks around the table. Jase isn't offended in the slightest when she stops next to him.

"I'll take it any way I can get it," Jase teases as he stands up and folds Mila in a tight embrace.

Seconds later, Mila's arms wrap around him, and I notice how she grips fistfuls of his shirt. They stand for so long it's well past the point of being just a hug.

When Mila finally pulls back, she ducks her head low, so her hair falls across her face, and hightails it back to her seat.

Ryker presses the button next, probably to draw our attention away from his sister, and a moment later, the arrow stops on Kao.

Admit how you feel to the person you like most.

"What happens if I don't take the dare?"

"You have to down a drink," I give him an out. We know Kao has feelings for Fallon, and I don't think this is the place for them to have *that* talk.

Kao grabs Jase's drink and downs it in one gulp, then gets up and makes the arrow spin again. It stops on Ryker.

Give someone a compliment.

Ryker turns to Tristan. "It's about time you pull your head out of your ass and go after the girl."

"That doesn't sound like a compliment," Tristan chuckles.

"Oh, and I'm proud of you," Ryker quickly adds. He gets to his feet. "I have to meet Danny, but it was nice seeing you all again." Ryker reaches for Jase's phone and presses spin on the screen before he walks away.

The arrow points to Jade.

Virgin Yes/No

Jade lets out a burst of air and rolls her eyes. "Well, that's no secret. Everyone knows I'm still a virgin thanks to a certain someone who couldn't keep his nose out of my business."

My right eyebrow shoots up because I didn't know she was still one. It's been two years. Does that mean she hasn't dated since Brady?

Jade presses the button, and the arrow falls on Noah.

Do you have a secret crush?

"We can drink, right?" he asks, already picking up his tumbler. He downs the last of the liquid then gets the arrow turning again.

It slows to a stop on me.

Kiss your enemy.

Oh shit.

My eyes dart to Jade, who's staring at the dare with apprehension.

Figuring I'd just give her a quick peck on the lips to fuck with her, I get up and say, "A dare's a dare."

"No, you can drink," Jade quickly objects.

Reaching her side, the corner of my mouth curves up. I take hold of her shoulders and pull her up from the chair. "Payback's a bitch," I grumble, lowering my head to hers. I press my mouth to Jade's just as she brings her hands up to my biceps.

I expect to be pushed away or punched at the very least, but instead, Jade goes still against me. Her lips begin to tremble, and when I move my own, something unexpected happens.

Awareness of the woman she's become trickles through me. All our cruel words and intimidating touches sparked a flame that should've had us going down in a blaze of hatred, but instead, makes desire sizzle to life.

Jade must feel the same intensity between us because instead of fighting me off, she presses herself closer to me, and her lips part beneath mine.

I block out all my thoughts about what's happening between us, what it might mean, and what our friends will think. I kiss her until all rationality leaves me, and I become nothing more than a thundering heartbeat, conscious only of what I want to do with this woman. It feels like we're crashing around in a stormy sea.

God, her scent, and the feel of her body pressing against mine – heaven.

It makes tiny fireworks explode behind my eyelids, and ripples of pleasure rush over every part of me.

Blindly, my tongue finds its way into the warmth of her mouth, and our walls come crashing down around us. We stand in the ruins of the past two years, oblivious to how this kiss will change our future.

JADE

This can't possibly be a kiss. It feels like I've been drugged, my mind cloudy, and my feet swept from under me by the force of the desire taking over every part of me.

I've never felt anything like this before. It's addictive and so intense, it wipes out all my common sense.

Where I should be pushing Hunter away, my hands deceive me and find their way to his face, framing his jaw while my tongue mimics the sensual movements of his own.

Hunter's arms wrap around me, and one of his hands grips hold of the back of my neck. The intensity spikes and the sparks I feel zapping between us turn into something akin to an inferno.

I'm surrounded by his masculine scent, and I'm all too aware of his muscular body pressing against mine.

I've only ever kissed Brady, and where he was like a cool breeze on a summer's day, Hunter is the sun itself, scorching through me and threatening to leave ashes of me in his wake.

Brady.

The thought is sudden and harsh, clearing my mind in an instant. I yank back as shame rattles through my soul like a skeleton in the closet demanding to be acknowledged.

I failed Brady.

I've tainted every kiss he's ever given me. I've betrayed the love we shared and the precious memory of him, I've fought so hard to protect.

With my breaths racing over my lips, swollen from Hunter's kiss, my wide eyes sweep over our friends. They're staring at us with similar shocked expressions on their faces.

"Jade." Hunter's voice is raspy, and it makes my eyes dart to his face.

Seeing his confused expression only makes my own turmoil burst to life, and not knowing what else to do, I turn away from him and run toward the exit.

Rushing out the doors, the night air is cool on my heated skin, and it causes me to shiver.

What just happened?

Why didn't I push Hunter away?

Why did I kiss him back?

The betrayal I feel sharpens in my chest, and it makes my eyes blur with unshed tears.

How can I feel anything but hatred for Hunter after the part he played in Brady's death?

"Jade!" Hearing how close Hunter is behind me, I don't have time to steel myself for a face-off with him. He takes hold of my shoulder and comes to stand in front of me. There's no longer any confusion darkening his features, but only concern. "Are you okay?"

I manage to shake my head.

No.

No, I'm far from okay.

Hunter tries to pull me into a hug, but this time I push him away.

That's what you should've done when he kissed you!

It feels like I'm being torn between my guilty conscience and my confusion. The emotions Hunter made me experience were... were... I don't even have words.

"Let's talk about this," Hunter's voice gets through to me.

He can't know. You have to hide your feelings, Jade!

I force my eyes to meet his and praying to all that's holy that I'll be convincing, I say, "It was just a game. A stupid kiss. It meant nothing, Chargill. I've had better."

Not knowing how I'll get home, I walk toward the street. I don't get far before Hunter darts in front of me again, and grabbing hold of my shoulders, his eyes burn into mine as he says, "You've always been bad at lying, Jade. That kiss meant as much to you as it did to me."

It meant something to him?

The thought is fleeting, and being so close to him, the embers of desire stir back to life, but I'm too upset and manage to pull away from him.

"I'm done talking about it."

When I start to walk again, Hunter calls after me. "Where the hell are you going? It's almost midnight."

"I'll walk to the campus," I yell back.

"God, give me strength." The growl is the only warning I have, and then Hunter grabs hold of me and lifting me off my feet, he throws me over his shoulder.

"Hunter Chargill!" My shriek echoes into the night air, but it doesn't stop him from carrying me back to where the cars are parked. "I'm going to kill you!"

"You can kill me after I've taken you back to the dorm," he snaps, sounding as frustrated and angry as I feel.

The movement from being placed back on my feet makes a dizzying wave rush through me, and when my legs buckle, Hunter quickly takes hold of my arm. "What's wrong?"

I wait for my eyesight to come back then glare at him. "You manhandling me made the blood rush from my head."

Hunter opens the passenger door and shoves me into the seat. When he climbs in behind the steering wheel, I'm still glaring at him while wondering why I haven't punched him unconscious yet.

He must read my thoughts from my expression because he says, "Like I said, you can kill me after I get you home."

Crossing my arms over my chest, I stare out of the window, refusing to talk to him any further.

The drive back to the campus is excruciating. My mind keeps racing between the emotions Hunter woke in me with just one kiss, and the guilt it makes me feel.

Thankfully Hunter doesn't say anything until we stop in front of the dorm. He switches off the car and turns to look at me. "Can we talk now?"

"Hell no," I snap as I shove the door open. I get out of the vehicle as fast as I possibly can. Slamming the piece of steel shut behind me, I rush into the building.

I'm relieved when Hunter doesn't follow me inside. The last thing I have strength for is to be stuck with him in the suite all alone.

Reaching my room, I go straight for the shower. When the water is finally pelting down on me, my thoughts start to slow.

I can't believe I kissed Hunter like that. What got into me?

I feel numb as I dry off and slipping into a pair of sweatpants and a comfy t-shirt, I climb into bed. I yank the covers over my head and squeeze my eyes shut, but it only makes images of Hunter flash before my eyelids. How hot he looked tonight. How gorgeous his face was as he leaned down. How sexy his grin was right before he pressed his mouth to mine.

I let out a growl as I throw the covers back and stare up at the dark ceiling.

Conflicted feelings press down on my chest until it's hard to breathe.

"What have I done?"

Chapter 9

HUNTER

When I get back to the club, the others are already outside. Tristan took Hana home, so only Jase and Fallon climb in with me while Mila rides with Kao and Noah.

"Are you okay?" Fallon asks from the back seat.

"Yeah," I lie through my teeth. I'm so not okay. Between my mind and my heart, I don't know which one is a bigger mess right now. I don't know how to start processing everything that happened tonight.

"Well, that was one hell of a surprise," Jase mumbles under his breath.

I let out a sigh while keeping my eyes on the road ahead. "You can say that again."

"Is Jade okay?" Fallon asks.

"I don't think so." I focus my attention on driving as we near a crossing, then add, "She's pissed and will probably kill me as soon as we get home."

There's a moment's silence, then Jase voices the obvious, "But she kissed you back. I mean, we all saw it. You were both pretty hot and heavy back there."

"Jase," Fallon chastises him.

"But he's right," I reply. Frustration bubbles to the surface because I can't make sense of what happened. "I was only going to give Jade a peck, but … fuck … I have no idea what happened."

"We'll deal with it. I'm sure it will blow over," Fallon tries to offer some hope.

"Nothing just blows over where Jade is concerned," I mutter as I steer the car through the gates of Trinity. "And it won't help to worry about it either. I'll have to keep taking the blows as they come."

Fallon is only quiet until the vehicle is parked, and we're climbing out. "You shouldn't have to take any blows. This has to stop. And that kiss didn't come from nowhere. It's obvious you both have feelings for each other."

"Who knows," I mutter as we walk toward the entrance of our dorm. "Lately, everything's just fucking confusing." I can't bring myself to enter the building, and grumble, "I'm going to take a walk."

"You want some company?" Jase asks.

I nod at him. "Thanks."

"I'll go check on Jade." Fallon gives me a tight hug, then whispers, "I'm sorry you're going through this. I'm here for you and will do everything I can to help you resolve things with Jade."

"Thanks, Fallon." I press a kiss to the top of her head and watch her go inside.

Jase and I turn toward the trail that runs into the woods behind the campus.

"How do you feel?" Jase asks.

I glance around at the lamps lighting up the pathway and throwing shadows on the trees and shrubs, then admit, "Confused. Fuck." I let out an aggravated breath. "Actually, this whole situation is starting to piss me off."

Jase lets out a sigh. "Yeah, I would've lost my shit months ago."

"It's been two fucking years," I snap, letting all my frustration bubble to the surface as I open up to my best friend. "Two! God, how much more do I have to take?"

And now the damn kiss has gone and fucked even more with my mind.

"Honestly," Jase shakes his head and gives me a somber look, "I would've given up a long time ago. I understand Jade's grief for Brady, but it gives her no right to blame you."

"And no matter how many times I tell her I had nothing to do with Brady's death, she refuses to listen," I grumble.

We reach the lookout point at the end of the trail and stare at the night sky.

Jase tucks his hands into the pockets of his pants as a frown forms on his forehead. "I don't get it. You were always so close." He nibbles at his bottom lip as he thinks, then murmurs, "Maybe Jade's taking her pain out on you because deep down she feels you're the strongest out of all of us."

I consider Jase's opinion on the matter but shake my head. "I don't think so."

The sounds of the night fill the silence between us, while memories of the past two years flash through my mind. Yeah, we used to be really close, but all the fights have caused a lot of damage to our relationship, and deep down, I know things will never be the same between Jade and me again.

"It's fucking sad," I admit to Jase. "Sometimes, I still can't believe how bad things have gotten between us."

"Not for lack of you trying." Jase pulls his left hand out of his pocket and places it on my shoulder. "God knows you've tried, but Jade's out for revenge. I have a feeling things will just keep getting worse."

I cross my arms over my chest and lock eyes with my friend. "Yeah, I have the same feeling, but I've reached the end of my rope with her."

"What are you going to do?" Jase glances out over the dark landscape.

"She wants revenge," I murmur, and as Jase brings his gaze back to mine, I state, "I'll make it so damn sweet she'll be begging for more."

If Jade hated me so much, then why did she kiss me back? Was it to play with me?

The thought only makes my anger grow because she's fucked enough with my heart. I seriously can't take more.

"You're not going to back off?" he asks.

Deep in thought, I shake my head. "A man can only take so much before he's had enough, and I reached my limit a while back. Jade started this war."

Jase worries his bottom lip again, then whispers, "And you plan on finishing it."

Nodding, I stare into the night. "It's time to end things between Jade and me."

Before, there's nothing left of my heart.

JADE

I've been lucky so far and haven't seen Hunter this morning. When Kao opens the door for Miss Sebastian, I let out the breath I've been holding, knowing I can relax while she's around. Hunter won't try to talk to me in front of my godmother, and I'm so not ready to face him after the kiss. I'm still trying to figure out why I kissed him back.

"My angel-children," Miss Sebastian practically croons as she first hugs Kao, then Noah and Mila. When she gets to me, I school my face, so none of my worries show. Miss Sebastian is like a dog with a bone when she catches whiff that one of us might have a problem.

"How was everyone's first week?" she asks. We all ramble an answer, then she says, "Show me around this bedazzled monstrosity of a campus, then we can go eat something."

Mila glances down at the glittering purple heels Miss Sebastian is wearing. "Did you bring a comfortable pair of shoes for all the walking?"

Miss Sebastian looks down at her feet, then frowns at Mila. "These are comfortable."

131

My eyebrow pops up, and I mumble, "Yeah, I'd probably break something if I had to wear shoes like that."

"No pain, no gain," Miss Sebastian quips. "Also, the mother of all fashion will curse my bedazzled ass if I stomped around in anything less than perfect shoes."

Miss Sebastian's clothing is extravagant and glittering, and it only adds to her larger than life personality. My dad and Kao's father helped Miss Sebastian go for a sex reassignment surgery before I was born. To me, she's always just been Mamma G, my larger than life fairy godmother.

I let Mila and Kao do most of the talking as we show Miss Sebastian around campus. When we reach the gym, a broad smile stretches across her face. "Abs for days."

"Hunter!" Hearing Melinda's screech, all our heads whip in their direction.

Seeing Hunter sends a sudden tremble through my body, and it doesn't help that he looks way too hot after being at the gym. There's still beads of sweat glistening on his skin... and his muscles... sigh... all the hotness in the world wrapped in a neat bow of deceit.

The same emotions I felt last night when we kissed hit me full force, and I quickly turn my head away from the group before someone sees it written all over my face. I can only hope it's temporary insanity brought on by the shock of having Hunter's mouth on mine.

Melinda stalks up to Hunter and shoves her pointer finger in his face. "You still owe Jessica an apology for last week."

"Oh, dear, who's the fashion disaster?" Miss Sebastian asks.

"She's a royal pain in my butt," I mutter under my breath.

Mila glares at Melinda and her three friends. "They're our nemeses."

My eyes dart to Mila as she walks over to where Hunter is staring at Melinda with an aggravated expression.

Melinda notices Mila first, and sneers, "Oh, look. Another one of your dogs that you can't keep on a leash."

"Say what now?" Miss Sebastian's perfectly manicured eyebrows almost disappear into her hairline, and then she darts forward.

Fallon, you're missing out on the showdown.

A smile tugs at the corner of my mouth as our godmother stops next to Mila.

"Did you just call my angel-baby a dog?" Miss Sebastian gives Melinda an incredulous look.

Melinda's lips pull down as her eyes sweep over Miss Sebastian then she turns her gaze to Mila. "How did you get into this prestige academy with a drag queen for a godmother?"

Her question burns over me, and anger explodes through me. With my eyes burning on Melinda, I stalk over to her, and just before I reach her, I pull back my arm. When my fist connects with her jaw, the feeling isn't nearly satisfying enough.

Melinda staggers backward, her eyes wide with shock. She's still gasping for air, her eyes brimming with tears when Hunter closes in on her. He crowds her personal space, a thunderous look tightening his features. "Pack your bags and get off my campus. You have one hour."

"What?" Melinda shrieks. "Jade just hit me, and I have to leave? That's unfair!"

"We do not tolerate discrimination in any form," Hunter bites the words out. "You have one hour, then I'll have you escorted off the grounds."

Two red spots bloom on Melinda's cheeks as the first tear rolls down her face. "My father won't be happy!"

Hunter looks up to the heavens as if he's praying for patience. "I don't care what your father thinks." Making a show of looking at his watch, his eyes snap back to Melinda. "You now have fifty-five minutes."

Melinda's eyes dart over the crowd that has formed around us, then they're back on Hunter with burning rage. "You can't expel me, Hunter. Trinity Academy doesn't belong to you."

"Oh, but he can," Jase's voice sounds up, and then he appears through the crowd. Placing his hand on Hunter's shoulder, he leans against him, then settles a bored look on Melinda. "Have you forgotten who his father is?"

"So, what if he's Mason Chargill's son? He's just the president."

I wrap my arm around Miss Sebastian's waist and hug her to my side. What Melinda said was cruel, and I really hope Hunter forces her off the campus. We'll have one less bitch to deal with then.

Hunter surprises me as he lets out a dark chuckle that makes goosebumps ripple over my skin. The sound is both hot and dangerous.

"Have you forgotten what my father did to the Weinstocks?" His eyes are icy, a clear sign that he's about to lose his temper. "I'm my father's son, and I won't hesitate to do the same to you."

"This is getting out of hand," Miss Sebastian says, hurt staining her always cheerful voice. "It's okay, Hunter."

Hunter's eyes snap to Miss Sebastian. "No!" Lifting his hand, he pinches the bridge of his nose and takes a couple of deep breaths. "Sorry, Miss Sebastian. I didn't mean to snap at you." Glaring at Melinda again, he growls, "You now have forty-five minutes."

Melinda's eyes dart over everyone. "I'll be back with my father, and you'll pay for degrading me in front of the student body."

I watch her walk away before I turn to Miss Sebastian. "Are you okay?"

She gives me a smile. "Yeah, she didn't say anything I haven't heard before."

Shaking my head, I wrap my arms around her and hug her tightly. "She's just a mean person. You always look beautiful."

"What Jade said." Jase moves to her side and wraps his arm around her. "You're a MILF."

Miss Sebastian's eyes grow huge before she bursts out laughing. "Mother of fashion!"

Embarrassment colors Jase's face a shade of pink, then he quickly tries to rectify himself. "I didn't mean it literally. I just meant you're beautiful and most probably star in a lot of men's fantasies."

"Not any better," Mila cries.

I begin to laugh and struggle to say, "Jase has a one-track mind."

When Miss Sebastian catches her breath, she flutters her eyelashes at Jase. "I never knew you had the hots for me, my chunk of hunk, but I'm a married woman."

Jase lets out a chuckle, knowing she's only teasing him. "I'm never going to live this moment down."

"Nope." Mila shakes her head at him with a warm smile and a proud look on her face. "But, you meant well."

My eyes dart to Jase, and I watch as Mila's words wash over him. His eyes are glued to her, and for a moment, I swear I can see love shining from them before he clears his throat and mutters, "I have to be somewhere."

My gaze follows Jase until Hunter's harsh voice gets my attention. "Are you waiting for something?"

I follow the direction of his cold eyes and see Jessica and her remaining two friends quickly shake their heads before they scatter into the dispersing crowd.

Miss Sebastian places her hand on my arm, and asks, "Is your hand okay? You gave her quite the punch. I thought her legs were going to fly right over her head."

I glance down at my knuckles and wiggle my fingers. "I'm fine. Tough as nails." I grin at my favorite person. "One punch wasn't enough, though. I should've removed some of her teeth."

"Aww, my little violent baby girl. You warm my heart," Miss Sebastian croons.

"I'm hungry, let's go eat," Kao says.

"Yes! Yummy food."

Miss Sebastian links her arm with his, and I watch them walk away before I look back to Hunter. He stood up for Miss Sebastian in a heartbeat, and it reminds me of the old Hunter who used to be my friend.

"Thank you for defending Mamma G," I mumble awkwardly, then I dart after my friends to catch up with them.

Chapter 10

HUNTER

After an eventful couple of days, I'm looking forward to spending a quiet day with my family. Jase, Hana, Fallon, and I are heading to Fallon's house for a BBQ. When Jase pulls up the driveway, I see my parents' car, where it's parked behind Uncle Lake's.

"Looks like our parents are all here," Jase states as he brings his vehicle to a stop.

"I hope they've started grilling the steaks," Hana says as we climb out. "I'm starving."

"That's if your father hasn't eaten it all already," Fallon teases.

When we walk into the house, we hear Uncle Lake's laughter, and then he screams, "Save me, Falcon."

"Don't hide behind Falcon," Dad shouts before I hear him laughing. "Hold still, you little shit."

Walking into the living room, I burst out laughing when I see Dad's straddling Uncle Lake and beating him with one of the scattered pillows. "I see nothing has changed," I say as I quickly greet my aunts.

Sitting down between Mom and my little sister, Aria, I throw my arms around their shoulders. Chuckling, Mom shakes her head, then says, "They'll never stop horsing around."

"And you all want to know why I like beating up, Hunter," Aria teases.

I ruffle her hair because I know my little sister hates it. "I let you beat on me so I can see if you can protect yourself."

Playfully sticking her tongue out at me, she taunts, "Excuses, excuses."

Dad finally gets up and drops the pillow on Uncle Lake, who's trying to catch his breath. Dad locks eyes with me and gestures with his head for me to follow him.

I join him out on the veranda and wait to hear what he wants to talk about.

For a moment, Dad just stares at me, then he asks, "Did Melinda Roberts deserve to be kicked off campus?"

"Damn," I let out a whistle, "I didn't expect them to call you so quickly." Dad tilts his head and lifts an expectant eyebrow, which has me explaining, "She insulted Miss Sebastian, calling her a drag queen. I think the punishment fits the crime."

Dad's eyes narrow. "She did what?" A second later, he holds up his hand. "No, don't repeat it." Stalking to the glass doors, he yells, "Julian, come here quickly."

Uncle Julian comes out with a tumbler in his hand. "You called?"

"You can tell Roberts to go fuck himself. His daughter insulted Miss Sebastian in the worst way. She can be lucky she only got expelled. I should get Preston to hack their bank accounts and close them."

I let out a chuckle because that would be awesome. Preston is Dad's assistant, and he's badass when it comes to all things computer-related. He's also the person who cleans up after me whenever I get in trouble. Not that it happens a lot, but it offers me peace of mind knowing he's there.

Uncle Julian takes a sip of whiskey, then states, "Then it's solved. I'll have Stephanie advise him to back down."

Uncle Julian heads back inside, and when I look at Dad, I see the pride shining from his eyes. "I'm glad to hear you stood up for her. She's a dear family friend."

"It's the least I could do." Throwing my arm around his shoulders, I joke, "But not half as badass as what you would've done."

Dad lets out a chuckle, then says, "Let's get this fire started before your Uncle Lake starts complaining that he's starving."

Dad's way of getting the fire going is to pour us each some whiskey while I light the wood. He pulls two chairs closer, and as we take a seat with our tumblers, the rest of the gang joins us outside.

Laughter continually fills the air, and it acts as a soothing balm to my battered heart after all the conflict I had to face this past week.

"Let's play a game," Jase says as he jumps up from his chair.

"My fucking heart," Dad yells, almost dropping his whiskey.

"He has a bad habit of doing that," I mutter.

Uncle Lake chuckles, then asks, "Which game did you have in mind?"

"Volleyball?" Jase asks. "We can play parents against the kids?"

"I've already used all my energy to fight off, Mason," Uncle Lake complains.

"Chicken," Jase mumbles under his breath, and it has Uncle Falcon and my Dad looking at him with raised eyebrows.

"Is that a dare?" Dad asks.

"Yep." Jase looks way too confident for my liking. My dad and his friends grew up on the beach, surfing and being more active than we've ever been.

"Let's do this." Uncle Falcon gets up and rolls up the sleeves of his dress shirt.

"You're going to play in a suit?" I ask, hoping for an excuse to get out of the game.

I'm not afraid to admit my father is stronger than me, and he'll probably wipe the floor with me.

"Yeah, come on, little Chargill," Uncle Falcon taunts.

"Oh, I see how it is," I grin as I get up. I shrug out of my jacket and drop it on the vacated chair.

Our parents only outnumber us with one person. The girls stand close to the net while the guys form a half-circle around them.

"Remember the rules," Uncle Julian calls out.

"Yeah, there are no rules," Jase chuckles as he sends the ball flying into the air towards his father.

But Uncle Lake jumps high, blocking the ball before he smacks it so hard it flies right over our heads.

"Scooooorrrre!!!!!" He jumps on Dad and Uncle Falcon, who gives my team smug grins.

"Just a lucky shot," Forest grumbles as he tosses the ball to Jase, who immediately serves before the other team is ready.

I let out a bark of laughter as Aunty Lee starts shouting in Korean, "Omeo! Omeo!" She ducks just as my mom dives forward, managing to hit the ball.

"Badass, Mom," I call out. My little sister hits the ball back, and soon we might as well be watching a tennis match between Mom and Aria.

"I'm hungry," Uncle Lake complains, and then he walks toward the grill.

"Yeah, me too," Jase agrees, following right behind him.

We all head back to the veranda, leaving Aria and Mom to battle it out.

It's only when I glance back that I notice Forest standing on the sidelines, his eyes not leaving Aria.

"He keeps saying they're just best friends," Fallon suddenly talks from next to me.

"Yeah?" Aria sneaks a look at Forest and her already flushed face, reddens more. "You think our siblings are more than friends?"

"It would be awesome, don't you think?" Fallon wraps her arm around my waist. "That way, we'll be in-laws."

"Only time will tell," I muse. My gaze goes back to Forest, and seeing the affectionate expression on his face makes me smile.

I'd thank my lucky stars if I can get Forest for a brother-in-law. Then I won't have to worry about my little sister and all the perverts out there when she starts at Trinity next year.

Fallon turns to face me, then says, "I managed to talk to Colton. He said he'd be in town soon, then he'll talk with Jade."

I tilt my head and give Fallon an apprehensive look. "I still don't think that's a good idea. Sometimes it's best to leave sleeping dogs lie."

"This war between you and Jade is the furthest thing from a sleeping dog."

"What about a sleeping dog?" Uncle Lake suddenly asks.

"Oh, nothing," Fallon says quickly, then she grins at Uncle Lake. "Nice goal."

I go take my seat next to Dad, and while my family and friends make jokes and their laughter form a protective bubble around me, I can't help but feel there's a storm coming.

JADE

After the hectic weekend, I spend my Monday afternoon working on my assignments, so I don't fall behind.

I've decided to study toward an MBA, so I can join the family business and work alongside my dad. Hana's the only one out of the four of us who's studying law, just like her father did.

There's a soft knock at my door, and then Fallon peeks into the room. "Hey, are you busy?"

Shaking my head, I smile at her. "Just working on an assignment. What's up?"

Entering, she shuts the door behind her, then takes a seat on the edge of my bed. "I wanted to talk to you about something."

I turn in my chair, so I can face her.

"First, hear me out, okay." She takes a deep breath and waits for me to nod before she continues, "I've contacted Colton, Brady's older brother."

"Wh–" After Brady's death, I tried to contact Colton and Mrs. Lawson, but their numbers must've changed, and after a while, I gave up.

Holding up a hand, she stops my question. "Let me explain before you ask questions." The serious expression on her face has worry niggling at my insides. "This thing between you and Hunter is starting to affect the whole group. It's time to find out what really happened when Hunter took Brady home. I asked Preston, Uncle Mason's brainy assistant, to find Colton. Colton has agreed to come and talk with you. I really think you should see him so you can get closure on what happened."

I stare at Fallon with wide eyes while her words shudder through me with both a sense of relief and apprehension. "Ahh…" I'm a little overwhelmed and first need to process all of this. Getting up, I go to sit next to Fallon.

She must see the nervousness written all over my face because she reaches for my hand. "If you want, I'll go with you to meet Colton."

"You've already done so much," I whisper. I finally manage to work through the initial shock and try to smile at my friend. "Thank you for finding him. I tried to contact him but figured he changed his number. Did he say when we'll be able to meet?"

Fallon shakes her head. "He said he'd call when he gets into town, but I'll forward you his number so you can get in touch with him."

I nod, and as the reality of Fallon's words sink in a weird emotion wiggles its way into my heart. It's along the lines of unease.

"I just wanted to let you know, so you're not caught off guard. I'll let you finish your assignment." Fallon gets up but then pauses. "Are you okay?"

I nod and force a smile around my lips. "Yeah, it's just a weird feeling knowing I'll hopefully get some answers for all my questions."

Fallon gives me a supportive smile. "I think it will be best so you can move on."

"You're right." Getting up, I give Fallon a hug. "Thank you."

"Sure." As she pulls back, she asks, "Are we still starting *Smallville* tonight, or do you need a raincheck?"

"Mila will kill us if we postpone. She wanted to start watching the series last Monday already."

Chuckling, Fallon agrees, "Yeah, let's not risk our lives. I'll go to the store for some snacks so we can pig out while drooling over Clark Kent."

"Great. I'll finish up here."

When Fallon leaves my room, I sit down by my desk again and stare at my laptop.

Will I finally get answers?

My mind is whirling with all the questions I have. Did Brady leave a letter behind? What happened when Hunter dropped off Brady at home? Were there any signs before Brady committed suicide?

I need to know the truth, but a nervous feeling spins a web in my stomach.

What if there were signs and I didn't notice them? What if I could've stopped Brady, but I didn't? What if it's my fault and Hunter really didn't have anything to do with it?

Chapter 11

JADE

The couple of times I've seen Hunter around the suite or campus, he didn't try to talk to me. Lucky for me because I'm too busy worrying about meeting with Colton to think about the kiss or anything else for that matter. Yesterday I got Colton's number from Fallon, and now I'm staring at my phone, feeling anxious as I read our short conversation.

Me: Hi, Colton. It's Jade. I got your number from Fallon Reyes. Can I call you?

Colton: I'll be in town today and will stop by Trinity. Face to face will be best.

Me: Ok.

I haven't heard anything since the messages, and even though I'm tempted to call Colton, I don't want to come across as being pushy. I'll give him time, and if I haven't heard from him by the end of the day, I'll make the call.

For now, I need to focus on school. Having to stop by the library for the *Ethics in Economics* book, I asked them to keep for me, I tuck my phone in my pocket and grab my keycard for the suite. I walk out of my room toward the living room but slow a little when I see Hunter and Jase sitting on the couch.

Jase lets out a holler, thrusting his fist into the air. "Yasssss!" Then he pats Hunter on the shoulder and holds out his hand. "Pay up."

Hunter pulls his wallet from his pocket and retrieves a couple of dollars. Shoving it in Jase's hand, he grumbles, "That was all luck."

I do my best to not make eye contact with Hunter and instead glance at the TV screen.

Seeing that they're watching reruns of Jeopardy, I ask, "What are you betting on?"

Jase grins at me. "Who will win. Hunter keeps losing."

I nod as I say, "If you see Mila, will you tell her I'm at the library? She's waiting for a book to be returned. If she wants me to check, she can shoot me a message."

"Why don't you just call her?" Jase asks while he tucks his winnings in his pocket.

"She's in class at the moment, but I did send her a text." Walking to the front door, I wave without looking at the guys in fear that I'll accidentally lock eyes with Hunter. "See you later." Slipping out of the suite, I let out a deep breath.

"That wasn't awkward at all," I mumble to myself as I walk to the elevator. Knowing I won't have to see Hunter for as long as I'm at the library, the tension eases out of my body.

I know at some point I'll have to face the fact we kissed, but if I have my way, it won't be happening anytime soon.

I walk out the building, and while glancing around, I turn toward the Library. It's a beautiful day out, and there's even a breeze in the air to help keep the heat at bay. Walking through the park, I take my time, so I can enjoy being outside and because I'm in no hurry to go back to the suite.

After getting the book, I'll head over to the restaurant for an early dinner, and then I can take a walk down one of the trails. That will buy me a couple of hours.

Trying to come up with things I can do so I don't have to see Hunter for the rest of the day, surprise ripples through me when someone grabs hold of my arm. "Jade."

My eyes dart to the face of the person talking to me, and then recognition dawns on me. "Colton." My voice is high-pitched with shock. Even though he agreed to meet, I didn't actually expect him to show up. "You came." I don't mean for it to sound like a question, but I'm filled with disbelief that Colton's standing in front of me after all this time.

Colton leans in and gives me a hug, and when he pulls back, he says, "Yeah, I was on my way to your dorm. I'm sorry I didn't contact you sooner."

"I tried to call you after the funeral," I say, a nostalgic pang hitting me square in the chest. Looking at Colton, I catch glimpses of Brady's face, and it only makes sadness bleed through me. I was starting to forget what Brady looked like, and I didn't even notice.

Glancing around, I spot a bench, and I gesture toward it. "Let's go sit."

Reaching the bench, I take a seat and wait for Colton to do the same before I ask, "How have you been? How are your parents?" I keep staring at the likeness of Brady I see in Colton's features.

"My mom's getting there. Brady's death hit her hard. At first, she was focused on getting us settled in the new house, but then she slipped into a deep depression." he says, sorrow tainting his voice. "The only good thing that happened the past two years is that my mom finally divorced that asshole excuse for a father we had. Your friend, Fallon, said you wanted to know what happened the night Brady passed?"

"Oh, I'm sorry your parents got divorced." Hearing how hard things have been for the Lawsons, makes me feel guilty for not trying harder to reach out to them. They suffered a tragic loss as well. "I didn't want to ask you any questions at the funeral, and a couple of weeks afterward, I couldn't get a hold of you," I explain my silence even though it now just feels like a selfish excuse.

Colton takes a deep breath and sadness trembles in his eyes. "We changed our numbers when we cut all contact with my father." He shakes his head and resting his elbows on his knees, he stares down at his hands.

I can see this is hard for Colton, and I don't want to push him for answers, so I sit patiently by his side and wait for him to open up to me about the happenings of that night.

After a long moment of silence, Colton shakes his head. "I should've protected Brady more. It's just… I was so fucking tired myself."

Colton's words only make more questions pop into my head, but I bite them back.

"Since birth, Brady was the sensitive one, and he took it so much harder than me," Colton admits. Bringing his gaze to mine, he explains, "Our father wasn't the loving parent you always saw whenever you paid us a visit. He never missed a chance to let us know how pathetic he thought we were. After you and Brady started dating, things got worse. He'd constantly rant at Brady, telling him he'd never be good enough for you." Colton pauses for a moment. "Brady started believing everything the old man spewed at him, no matter how hard I tried to tell him any different."

The news doesn't hit me like a lightning bolt. Instead, it feels like I'm slowly being drowned. It's becoming harder to breathe as pain fills my chest. "Mr. Lawson was abusive?" I ask for clarity.

Colton nods. "He never got physical, but damn, sometimes I think it would've hurt less if he'd just hit us, instead of laying into us with his rants of how useless we were."

Hearing Brady was abused is breaking my heart all over again. He was so sweet and wouldn't hurt a fly. Tears well in my eyes and unable to stop them, they spill over my cheeks.

"I'm so sorry," I whisper, my voice hoarse from the overwhelming feelings. I know the full impact of Colton's words hasn't hit me yet. It feels like I'm stuck in the calm before the storm. "I wish I had known. I would've tried to help."

Colton lets out a deep breath and glances at me. Seeing my tears, he awkwardly places an arm around my shoulders. "We didn't want anyone to know. Back then, we both believed we were worthless."

Brady ended his life because he didn't feel like he was worth anything?

Oh, my God.

I suck in a painful breath before I say, "He meant everything to me. I loved Brady with all of my heart. Didn't he know that?"

Slowly Colton rubs his hand over my back. "He knew, Jade. He just couldn't handle the abuse any longer. It broke him."

Lifting my hand to my face, I cover my mouth to muffle the sob escaping my lips.

Brady was always so loving toward me. I try to remember our time together, but still, I can't find any signs that Brady was being abused at home.

"What happened the night he... he..." I can't bring myself to say the words.

Colton pulls his arm back and rests his elbows on his knees again. Staring out over the campus, he says, "When Brady got home from the party, he was upset."

What did Hunter do to upset Brady?

Before I can voice the question, Colton continues, "We were in our room. Brady admitted to me that you were ready to take your relationship to the next step."

My eyes widen, and I shift uncomfortably on the bench.

"He didn't believe he deserved a girl like you. I tried to tell him he did and that your feelings for each other were all that mattered."

I wipe a trail of tears from my cheek. It feels like my heart is splitting right down the middle. Back then, all I thought about was having sex with Brady, and not once did I consider that he might not be ready.

I close my eyes against the pain the realization causes.

"Our dad overheard the conversation, and he laid into Brady again." Colton sucks in some air and lightly shakes his head. "I should've stayed at home, but I got so angry and not wanting to make things worse, I left." Colton brings his devastated eyes to mine. "If I had stayed at home that night, Brady would still be here."

157

I shake my head and impulsively wrap my arms around Colton, hugging him. "It was your father's fault," I try to console him.

And Hunter's.

I'm about to ask the question when Colton pulls back and shakes his head at me. "It was also my mother's fault and mine. We all knew he was an abusive bastard, but none of us did anything. We all worked our asses off to hide our dirty family secret."

Knowing Colton needs to hear the words, I say, "Brady loved you so much. He always said how lucky he was to have a big brother like you."

"Some big brother I was." Colton chokes on the words, and my hand darts up to pat his back. "I wasn't there when he needed me most. I left him to deal with that asshole all alone."

"I'm so sorry, Colton," I whisper. "I can't begin to imagine how bad things were. I should've seen the signs as well."

We sit in silence with our guilt and loss.

Knowing I could've done something to help Brady if only I had known, eats away at my soul. My tears dry up because I have no right to shed them. I let a loved one down, and it makes me wonder what else I've been blind to in my life.

I'm filled with numbing heartbreak and disappointment in myself as a human being.

Colton gets up, and a weak smile tugs at the corner of his mouth. "I'm sorry I didn't tell you sooner. I know it doesn't offer much closure, but I thought you should know why Brady committed suicide."

I rise to my feet and nodding, I give his arm a squeeze. "Thank you. I really appreciate it. Are you going to be in town for a while? I'd like to meet up for coffee or dinner."

Colton shakes his head. "I'm heading to Los Angeles for a meeting and then back home. But you have my number. Let's stay in contact this time."

I nod and struggle to keep the tears back as Colton leans down and folds me in a hug. "You were the best thing that happened to Brady," he whispers.

Through a blur of pain, I try to smile at Colton. "Thanks for coming." The words are thick, and my throat is starting to ache from the fight to not break down in front of Colton.

"I have to go, but I hope you're happy here." He glances around the campus again, and I take the moment to look at his face.

Same soft brown eyes as Brady.

Same brown hair.

Same sad lines tugging at his smile.

It's a battle to keep a smile around my trembling lips, and as Colton begins to walk away, it falters as I remember my question about Hunter. "Colton," I call out, needing to ask him what part Hunter played in Brady's suicide.

He glances back over his shoulder. "Yeah?"

"What happened when Hunter dropped Brady off at home? Did Brady say anything?"

Colton thinks back and shakes his head. "Nothing happened. It was nice of Hunter to give Brady a ride home, though."

My mouth dries up at his answer. "So, Hunter didn't fight with Brady?" I ask to make sure.

Again, Colton shakes his head. "Not at all. Why? Did something happen at the party to make you think Hunter would pick a fight with Brady?"

"He walked in on us where we were alone in a bedroom," I explain.

"Brady mentioned that, but he wasn't upset about it. Truth be told, he was relieved because he didn't have to tell you about our dad."

Frowning, I ask, "So Brady would've told me about the abuse if we weren't interrupted?"

"No, Jade." Colton gives me a sympathetic smile. "Brady couldn't tell you, and it was killing him. He didn't want you to look at him with pity."

I nod as my heart takes a final blow. "I understand."

"Look after yourself, Jade."

"You too." I watch Colton walk away and let wave after wave of heartache crash over me.

Brady was hurting so much, and I never saw it. How could I be so blind? My mind turns to Hunter, and the blood drains from my face.

I blamed him for so long, and he was telling the truth.

Oh, my God.

I ruined our friendship over something that was never Hunter's fault.

HUNTER

I just lost another fifty dollars to Jase, but seeing how excited he gets when he wins has me agreeing to the bets.

161

"The blonde woman's going to kick ass," Jase says, his eyes glued to the TV.

"Hunter's already lost two hundred dollars. Shouldn't you guys stop now?" Fallon asks from where she's sitting by the kitchen counter, having a yogurt.

I wink at her, then joke, "He's on a mission to drain my bank account. There's no stopping Jase now."

"You bet your ass," Jase hollers as the blonde woman gets an answer right. "Yasss, mamma. Show them how it's done."

Fallon points at me with her spoon. "You're creating a gambling addict."

I let out a bark of laughter, and I'm just about to tease her when the front door opens, and Jade walks in. I only glance at her for a split-second, and her presence instantly puts a damper on my good mood.

Whenever I see her around the suite or on campus, I'm reminded of the damn kiss and how it felt to hold her in my arms. But seeing as I'm still dealing with the emotions myself, I haven't pushed Jade to talk about what happened.

"Are you okay?" Fallon asks. It makes my head snap back to Jade, and it's only then I see her red-rimmed eyes and how pale her face is.

Jade's stunned-looking gaze meets mine, and she opens her mouth, but no words come out.

Jase switches the TV off and rises to his feet, a concerned look chasing away the glow of fun he had. I also get up as Fallon walks closer to Jade, asking, "Jade, what's wrong?"

Jade moves her gaze to Fallon, then back to me, and it makes apprehension grow inside of me.

Please, God, let it not be serious.

I've just sent up the silent prayer when Jade says, "I-I met with Colton Lawson."

"I didn't know you were meeting with him today," Fallon exclaims. "How did it go? Did you get any answers?"

Jade nods, her eyes never leaving mine. "He told me why Brady committed suicide." Tension ripples through my body, tightening all my muscles as I wait for the blow. "They were abused by Mr. Lawson." A sharp breath prevents her from talking, and she tears her eyes away from me, looking at Fallon. "Brady was being abused, and I didn't even know. How did I not see the signs? What kind of girlfriend does that make me?"

Fallon closes the distance between them and hugs Jade. "I'm so sorry, Jade. It's just awful."

163

Jade shakes her head as she pulls away. "I saw the pain on Colton's face. How could I not see it on Brady's?" Fallon wraps her arm around Jade's waist to offer her comfort.

When Jade brings her eyes back to me, there's no hatred or anger shining from them, and it's only then her words hit me.

Jade has finally learned the reason for Brady's suicide.

But I still need to hear her say it. I watch her swallow hard, and her voice is hoarse as she admits, "I'm so sorry, Hunter. I'm sorry for blaming you. I thought... I really thought... I..."

My mouth sets into a hard line, and the months of anger I've been suppressing bubbles to the surface like an erupting volcano. What happened to Brady is tragic, but damn, I waited two fucking years for an apology, and that's all she has to say?

Months of fighting, of heartbreak, of unfairness, blast through me, leaving me feeling exasperated and outraged.

Seeing the regret on Jade's face does nothing to make me feel better. "I'm so sorry," she repeats the empty words.

"So Brady's old man is responsible for him committing suicide?" Jase asks.

"Yes, he was verbally abusive and broke Brady and Colton down. Colton got angry that night and left Brady to face Mr. Lawson alone. Things got bad, and I guess Brady couldn't handle it anymore," Jade tells us what she knows. "It's horrible and so tragic. I should've known something was wrong. I should've been there for Brady."

Tears spill over her cheeks, and she gives me a pleading look. "Hunter... I..."

Jade first needs to deal with her grief before we talk about everything. I deserve more than a half-assed apology for all the times she's lashed out at me and disrespected me.

I shake my head and walk toward my room, not wanting to say anything I'll end up regretting.

"Hunter, please," she calls out as I reach my door, and it makes me pause for a moment. "I'm so sorry I blamed you."

I let out a breath then do my best to ignore her sob as I step into my room. Jase is right behind me, and he shuts the door to give us some privacy.

"Fuck," he lets out on a sigh. "Finally, we know the truth."

Swinging around, my eyes lock on him as anger rages through me. "I always knew the truth! What? Now I have to pretend nothing happened the past two years and go back to the way things were? Fuck that."

Jase's expression sobers in an instant, and he closes the distance between us. "I didn't say that."

A frown darkens my forehead as I shake my head in disbelief. "What the fuck was that? An apology?" I begin to stalk up and down the width of my room, needing to release my emotions in some way.

"This whole situation sucks," Jase muses. "It just fucking sucks."

"Two fucking years!" The shout rips from me, and my breaths come faster. "She fucking attacked me every opportunity she got."

Sadness washes over Jase's features, and stepping in front of me to stop my pacing, he places his hands on my shoulders. "You have all the right to be angry. Let it out."

I shake my head, and my face is torn with the loss I've suffered, the torment I had to just bare, the blame I had to carry.

I shut my eyes for a moment, but they snap open when I hear the sound of my door clicking open. My eyes lock on Jade as she steps into my private space, and I grind the words out, "Get out. Now is not the fucking time."

"Hunter." Her voice is cautiously soft as she gives me a pleading look. "Can we please talk about it." I shake my head, but she must have a death wish because she doesn't back down. "I'm sorry I blamed you. I shouldn't have accused you."

"Jade, not now," Jase says, knowing the thunderous expression tightening my features means not to fuck with me.

"I just want to apologize," she says, her face filled with panic and guilt.

My eyes burn into Jade's as I slowly close the distance between us. I lift my hand and pressing against her shoulder, I shove her out of my room. "Mine was never good enough for you. There's no way in hell I'll ever accept yours."

I slam the door shut and make sure to lock it this time before I suck in a lungful of air.

I gave her time when she didn't deserve any. I let her take her anger out on me even though I did nothing wrong. I always thought when Jade learned the truth of that night, we would be able to go back to how things were between us.

But I was wrong.

There's nothing to go back to. Jade made sure of that.

Chapter 12

HUNTER

The immediate rage I felt at hearing why Brady committed suicide has subsided, leaving me feeling wronged and … just fucking drained.

It's been two days since Jade's so-called apology. I don't know if Jase or Fallon spoke with her because she's giving me my space.

Fallon and Hana have been working on getting everything ready for the ball tonight. Every year we have the function to welcome the students. It's actually just a get together so students can get to know each other, but the girls use it as an excuse to dress up.

The last thing I'm in the mood for is to be social tonight. I stare at the jacket lying on my bed and zone out as my thoughts return to the past.

'I hate you, and I wish it was you instead of Brady.'

Jade's words have become like a whip, lashing at the scars she's left in her wake.

'Don't ever call me again. You lost that right when Brady killed himself because of you. I hate you, Hunter Chargill.'

I can't even remember how many times she said she hated me. Or the number of times she wished I had died instead of Brady.

I have no words for how I feel. The closest I can get to the rampant feelings swamping me is tormented. Before the truth came out, I got frustrated whenever we fought, but now all the accusations and cruel words flash through my mind, taunting me. It infuriates me, stoking my anger.

'I'll never forgive you, Hunter. Someday I'm going to make you pay. I don't know how or when, but I promise you, you'll pay for what you've done to Brady.'

I let out a bitter chuckle as I reach for the jacket. Shrugging it on, I mumble, "Now it's your turn to pay, Jade."

I check my reflection in the mirror and stare at the furious expression on my face. I've never been good at hiding my feelings. Letting out a tired sigh, I straighten the jacket then walk over to my dresser so I can grab my

Rolex. Strapping it on, I look at the closed door and mutter, "It's going to be a long fucking night."

Knowing there's no way of getting out of attending the ball, I stalk to the door and yank it open. I force myself to not glance at Jade's door and walk to the living room. Jase and Noah are already sitting on the couch, ready for the evening.

"Looking good guys," Mila says as she comes up behind me.

I go to take a seat on one of the open sofas and smile at Mila. "Red really suits you. You look beautiful, Mila."

She grins at my compliment, and when her eyes dart to Jase, I glance at my friend. His lips are parted, and there's a mixture of wonder and heat in his stunned expression.

Clearing his throat, he blinks a couple of times, then mutters, "Yeah, you don't look too bad."

"Gee, thanks," Mila snubs him.

"Mila, can you help me with my necklace?" Fallon asks as she walks into the open space.

Kao is right behind her. "I'll help." He takes the delicate piece of jewelry and moves in front of her.

My eyebrows slowly rise as I watch Kao tenderly brush her hair to the side before he leans into her. He clasps the necklace in place, and I swear everyone is holding their breaths when he pauses with his cheek pressing against Fallon's.

Then he pulls back, and his eyes glide over the silver dress, which fits her perfectly. "You look breathtaking, Fallon."

Fallon's eyes drop from his, and she brings a hand up, fiddling with the single diamond resting on her neckline. "Thanks, Kao." A nervous smile, which is a rare sight when it comes to Fallon, graces her lips. "You almost look like an adult in the suit."

She darts around him and makes a beeline for me. I scoot closer to the armrest to make space for Fallon right before she plops down on the sofa. I can feel the tension coming off her in waves and rest my arm behind her on the couch.

She gives me a thankful look, then jokes, "There's still time to back out of going to the ball."

I let out a chuckle. "After all your and Hana's hard work, I wouldn't miss it for anything."

"My zip is stuck," Hana complains while she tries to reach behind her.

"Let me get it," Jade suddenly says from behind Hana as she walks into the living room. For a second time tonight, I hold my breath as my eyes scan over the light blue silk dress Jade's wearing. She's curled the tips of her ginger strands, and it makes the auburn in her hair pop out more.

She looks stunning, but hell will freeze over before I give her a compliment.

Jade fiddles with Hana's zip, and then gets it to go up. "There you go." She grins at Hana. "You look so pretty in pale pink. That's one color I'm allergic to with my red hair."

"Thanks, my friend." Hana glances over everyone then says, "Well, we're all ready. Let's go."

I rise to my feet and hold my hand out to Fallon to help her up then wait for her to walk ahead. When we reach Hana, she hooks her arm through Fallon's and says, "Oooh, the guys are going to go gaga over you tonight."

"They better not. I'll have Jade throat punch them all," Fallon jokes.

Jase falls in next to me, and we leave the suite with Kao, Noah, Mila, and Jade somewhere behind us.

It's a habit we learned at a young age — Fallon at the head with Hana in the middle, and then Jase and I behind them. Dad once explained to me it's because we always have to form a united front, and it's Jase and my duty to protect the girls at all cost.

JADE

Fallon asked me to give Hunter some time before talking to him about what happened, but damn it's hard.

After Colton came to see me, I was distraught over what happened to him and Brady. Now I'm left with regret.

A shit load of regret.

Knowing I failed Brady is something I'll just have to learn to live with, and I've come to realize there can never be any closure when it comes to a loved one taking their own life.

And then there's Hunter.

I'm angry with myself for screwing up so badly. I've been going over the week of Brady's passing, trying to remember what made me think Hunter was to blame. But I've got nothing.

My only defense is that I was a grief-stricken sixteen-year-old. Because I was upset with Hunter for interrupting Brady and me, I latched onto that anger.

But it's no excuse.

Walking next to Mila, my eyes are glued to Hunter's broad back.

Regret is actually an understatement for what I feel. I've single-handedly destroyed a friendship that meant the world to me. I was cruel and, at times, downright vile toward Hunter, and the fact that he never lashed out against me goes to show what an amazing person he really is.

An amazing person who I pushed away every damn chance I got.

Ashamed for my awful behavior, I know I have to do everything in my power to try to make things right between us.

Even if it takes two years to fix things between Hunter and me. I'll do anything I have to.

I deserve his anger because, at the end of the day, I hurt and insulted Hunter in the worst way possible.

When we walk into the hall, Mila and I head straight for our table while Fallon, Hana, Jase, and Hunter do their rounds at the tables to welcome all the students.

My gaze follows Hunter. He stops by Jessica Atwood and her posse of friends' table, and I frown when she says something to him with a rueful smile. My frown only deepens when she holds out her hand to him, and Hunter actually shakes it before moving onto the next table.

"Did you see that?" I ask Mila.

"Yep." She places her elbow on the table and rests her chin on her hand. "Looks like Jessica apologized to Hunter."

I give Mila a what-the-hell look. "She must be afraid of being kicked out after what happened to Melinda."

"Serves them right. Hopefully, it put them all in their place." Then Mila turns her head to Kao. "What happened to you and Summer coming together to this thing?"

Kao shrugs. "After the incident with Melinda, I thought it would be best to keep my distance from that group of girls. Besides, I'm hoping to dance with Fallon."

My eyebrows pop up. "Yeah? You're finally going to ask her to date you instead of eyeing her from a distance?"

Kao shakes his head, a sad smile tugging at his lips. "No, I just want to have one dance with her."

"You should tell her how you feel," Mila says.

Kao just shakes his head while his eyes drift to Fallon as she crosses the floor toward our table. "Let's drop the topic."

Fallon stops by the side of the table and pins Kao with a look that's filled with bravery. "Kao, will you please open the dance floor with me?"

Surprise flutters over his face, but he's up and walking toward her in a split-second, and it makes me struggle to not laugh.

I watch as he takes hold of her hand and leads her over to the floor. Their eyes lock as violin strings fill the air, and I feel the intensity all the way from where I'm sitting.

"You know, this is where Uncle Falcon and Aunty Layla's relationship started," Jase comments as he comes to stand behind Mila while *Secrets* by *One Republic* plays. "Maybe it's a good thing for Fallon and Kao."

"That would be awesome," I say, glancing up at Jase.

He holds his hand out to Mila and says, "How about we stop pretending we hate each other for a couple of minutes, and you dance with me?"

Mila glares at Jase, but still, she places her hand in his, grumbling, "You have one song."

"I'll take what I can get," Jase smiles as he leads her away from the table.

"Damn, is it just me, or is there love in the air?" Noah asks as he gets up to come to sit next to me.

"I'm hoping love is in the air," I reply, grinning because I'm happy to see my friends dancing, and I think the song fits them perfectly.

Hana slumps down in a chair and reaches for a bottle of water. "My shoes are killing me."

I wiggle my toes in the snug confinement of the heels I'm wearing. "I feel your pain." I grin at Hana. "Aren't you going to pick someone to dance with?"

Hana shakes her head, and her eyes turn to Fallon. "No, Fallon and Jase dancing is enough. Besides, there's no one here I want to dance with."

"Ouch." Noah slaps his hand over his heart, feigning hurt.

Hana lets out a chuckle. "My feet are in pain. I'd dance with you in a heartbeat, but I'd rather just sit here until this night is over."

"Just pulling your leg," Noah says with a grin.

I glance around at the colorful decorations and beautiful flowers. "The hall looks so pretty. You guys did a wonderful job."

"Thanks, but it's the first and last time I'm helping the decorating committee."

My eyes search for Hunter, and I find him at a table with Nate Sparks and his friends, which is surprising. Hunter laughs at something Nate says. I got the feeling Hunter didn't care for them much, but I must've been wrong.

Not surprising, Jade. You've been wrong about a ton of things.

On the spur of the moment, I get up and walk toward Hunter, hoping that if I asked him to dance, he wouldn't reject me in front of all the students. I know it's an underhanded way of trying to talk to him, but I'm scared if I let too much time pass, he won't give me a chance to apologize at all.

Nate sees me first, and his smile broadens. "Damn, you look good, Jade."

"Thanks." My eyes rest on Hunter's face, and it takes a couple of seconds before his gaze flicks up to meet mine. "Hunter, I was hoping you'd dance with me?"

His blue eyes turn to solid ice, and my hope quickly fizzles away. His features set into hard lines as he rises from the chair and buttoning his jacket, he leans a little closer to me, whispering, "Not in a million years."

The sharp edge to his tone sends goosebumps rushing over my skin, almost as if a chill just swept through the room.

He starts to walk away from me, but I dart after him, grabbing hold of his arm. Hunter stops, and his eyes are filled with disdain as they drop to where I'm touching him.

I quickly pull my hand back and say, "Please, can we talk?"

"You really want to do this here?" he snaps as he turns to face me. Before I learned the truth, my anger made me brave and reckless, but now I struggle not to cower back from the fury radiating from his body.

Before I can plead for his forgiveness, Hunter steps closer to me in one hell of an aggressive move, but I keep my ground.

"I've given you two years, Jade. I refuse to waste another second of my time on you." His words are harsh, but I know I deserve every one of them.

"I know, and I'm so sorry, Hunter. Can we go outside so you can tell me how you feel? I want to fix things between us."

He lets out a burst of air, the corner of his mouth pulling into a vicious grin I haven't seen before. "You want to know how I feel?"

I nod quickly, praying he'll open up to me.

Hunter pulls back, and his eyes lock on mine. They look cold and expressionless as he says, "At first I was angry and fucking upset, but then I realized it meant I cared. Now?" He shrugs carelessly. "Now, I feel nothing. You insulted me and went as far as repeatedly accusing me of murder. I guess I could retaliate, but I won't because I'm not that kind of person. We're done. There's nothing left of our friendship to salvage. You made sure to destroy what we had."

"Hunter," I plead as tears begin to sting my eyes, realizing I'm not going to get a chance to try to fix things between us. I grab onto the only splinter of hope I have left. "What about the kiss?"

Hunter lets out a dark sounding chuckle. "Like you said, Jade, it was just a kiss. A stupid game and probably the biggest mistake I've ever made. It meant nothing." He begins to turn away but then stops, and his tone is biting as he says, "One last thing, don't ever touch me again or pretend we're friends."

Chapter 13

HUNTER

Thanks to Jade picking such a shitty time to talk to me, everyone on campus now knows we're fighting after the scene that played out between us.

Back at the suite and finally done with the night, I shrug out of my jacket and rip the tie loose from around my neck. I toss the fabric on my bed and then freeze when a song begins to play loudly outside my room.

Fuck, I forgot to shut the damn door behind me.

For a moment, I listen to the words as *Fighting Gravity* by *Caleb Johnson* fills the air. When he sings, *'The memories are all I'll save tonight...,'* I swing around and stride to the door, slamming the thing shut in Jade's face.

The woman knows no end. I'll give her that. She doesn't know the meaning of giving up on anything.

'...never thought you would ever quit on me... Without you, I'm gasping, it's hard to breathe...'

The words are hard to hear because I lied to Jade in an attempt to hurt her as much as she hurt me. I don't think I have it in me to ever quit on her, no matter how many times I've said that I'm done with her.

'I hate you, and I wish it was you instead of Brady.'

Heartache splinters through me, and I close my eyes as they begin to burn from the tormenting memory. It hurts so fucking much it's becoming difficult to breathe. I take a gasp of air and sink to my knees from the overwhelming feelings weighing down on me.

'I hate you.'

"Fuck," I groan, grabbing at my shirt and fisting the fabric over my aching heart.

She fucking broke my heart over and over.

I don't even hear my door open and only realize Hana is in the room with me when she kneels in front of me.

"I'm here," she whispers, and when I lift my painfilled eyes to hers, a tear trails over her cheek. "It's okay to cry."

I shake my head and try to fight my emotions back, but they're too out of control. The heartache is too intense.

Hana lifts her hand to my cheek and gives me a sad smile. "I wish I could help you carry the hurt."

My body begins to shake from all the effort it's taking to not cry.

I hear the door behind me, and when Fallon asks, "Are you okay?" I can only shake my head.

She drops down next to me and wraps her arms around me, and it breaks the last of my resistance. I lower my head until it rests against Hana's shoulder and let the first tear fall.

It doesn't ease any of the pain. It doesn't wash away the anger. I don't find any release, but instead, it makes a pressure build up inside of me until it feels like I might explode.

Fallon tightens her arms around me, murmuring, "We're here. We've got you."

Every scathing word. Every punch. Every hateful look.

When I finally manage to reign in the tears, I pull back and ask, "How am I suppose to just forget what she did to me?"

Fallon brushes her hand over my cheek and shakes her head. "No one expects you to, Hunter. You need time to heal, and we all understand that."

"Can I even heal? It took all my strength to fight her. I don't think I have any left to forgive her."

With a world of wisdom way beyond her years, Hana smiles tenderly at me. "It takes time, Hunter. It's not something you can give overnight; otherwise, people would be handing it out left, right, and center. Forgiveness is the final stage of healing."

I nod, knowing she's right. I let out an exhausted breath. "I keep saying I'm done with her. Damn, I just said I don't think I can forgive her, but..." I move to get up, and when I start to pace the width of my room, the girls go to sit on my bed.

Fuck, all these emotions are giving me whiplash.

My voice is strained, when I say, "Jade's a part of our group, and even though our friendship took one hell of a knock, I can't bring myself to stop caring about her." I let out a bitter chuckle. "Fucked up, isn't it? I'm a sucker for fucking punishment."

"Not at all," Fallon says. "You can't just stop loving someone, Hunter. You've fought so hard for so long. You finally don't have to be the one to keep the peace. Jade took her grief out on you, and now that she's finally healing, you no longer have to be her rock. But now, you need time to deal with the heartache it caused you."

The corner of my mouth lifts slightly. "Jase said something similar the other day."

Fallon lets out a chuckle. "Yeah, he can be insightful when his mind's not in the gutter."

There's a moment of silence, then Hana asks, "Do you feel a little better?"

"Yeah." I give the girls a grateful smile. "I think I just had to admit the truth to someone."

"Do you want me to talk to Jade so she'll keep her distance until you're ready to talk to her?" Fallon asks.

"I got the impression you already did that, but Jade just chose not to listen?" I smirk because it's precisely something Jade would do.

"Yeah, I mentioned it to her, but this time I'll sit her down and explain that she needs to back off."

"I'd appreciate it. I just need to work through my emotions."

The girls get up and come to give me a hug. Pulling back, Hana's dark eyes search my face, and pleased with what she sees, she presses a kiss to my cheek.

When the girls leave to go talk to Jade, I go to take a shower. With the warm water easing the tension from my muscles, I feel much better when I'm done. I dry off and step into a pair of sweats.

Walking back into my room, I come to a stop when I see Jase stretched out on my bed.

"You're not sleeping here," I warn as I walk closer.

Jase turns on his side and grins at me. "Come on, I know you love snuggling with me. I won't tell anyone."

"Fucker," I chuckle as I poke at him to move up. "We're getting too old for this."

"Yeah, so enjoy it while it lasts. Once Mila gives in to me, you won't be seeing my ass at night."

"Can't fucking wait," I mutter as I climb under the covers. "And I swear if you fart, I'll kill you."

"*Eau De Jase*. People will pay millions to get a whiff," he jokes.

"In your dreams," I laugh. "You're nuclear. I'm sure NASA picks up whenever you detonate."

We chuckle, and it's just what I needed.

I reach for the bedside lamp and switch it off, then whisper, "Thanks, Jase."

"Always."

There's a moment's silence, then I say, "Love you."

"Love you most," he murmurs, already sleepy.

I lay awake, listening to Jase's light snoring, thinking about Jade.

I'm worried we won't be able to go back to how things were between us, but maybe once we've worked through our problems, we can start a new friendship. I just have no idea how we'll get there.

JADE

Last night Fallon had a serious talk with me, and it opened my eyes. I need to be as patient with Hunter as he was with me.

At this point in time, it's the least I can do.

I'm glad I have classes to keep me busy, but I constantly find my mind drifting to Hunter and everything I've put him through.

I let out another regretful sigh as my ethics lecture comes to an end. I've just closed my laptop when someone behind me pours liquid over my back. Some splashes onto my computer, and I rush to free tissues from my bag so I can quickly wipe it up before there's any damage.

"I'm so sorry," I hear Jessica apologize, and glancing over my shoulder at her, I watch as she takes one of her own tissues and pats my back. "I lost my balance, and my coke just spilled everywhere."

"It's okay," I mutter and proceed to pack my stuff away.

As I get up and begin to walk down the aisle, Jessica says, "Please send me the dry-cleaning bill."

"Don't worry about it," I call back to her.

I decide to go change my shirt before I go for lunch and walking into the suite, Hana's head pops up from where she was lying on the couch, watching a movie with Hunter. "You're back early?"

"Just changing my shirt. Jessica spilled her drink on me," I explain, using all my will power to not look at Hunter.

"On purpose?" Hana asks, sitting up with a frown.

"No, it was an accident." I rush into my room and quickly grab a fresh shirt. After shrugging it on, I take my laptop from my bag and open it to make sure it didn't get damaged by the fluid. I let out a sigh of relief when everything seems fine and closing the computer again, I tuck it back in my bag. "Time for food."

I keep my eyes trained in front of me, and as I pass by the living room, I call out, "Enjoy the rest of the movie."

"Thanks," Hana replies as I slip out of the door.

I hurry so I don't keep Mila waiting too long, but walking into the restaurant, someone bumps into me, and it sends me stumbling backward. I slam into something solid and glancing over my shoulder, I see that it's Jase.

189

"You okay?" he asks, but his eyes are boring into whoever bumped me.

"Yeah," I reply quickly and add, "It was an accident. I wasn't watching where I was going."

My explanation sets Jase at ease, and he steers me past Justin, who says, "Yeah, it was an accident."

"No worries." The last thing I want is Jase starting a fight because of me.

When we get to the table, I sink down on a chair and let out a breath while complaining, "I'm accident prone today."

"What happened?" Mila asks with a concerned look tightening her features.

"First, Jessica spills her drink on me, and then I walked into Justin."

"Oh." The single word doesn't make it sound like Mila's convinced they were accidents.

"Come on, lets order. I'm starving," I say to change the subject. "I think I deserve some pizza today, but I don't want a whole one."

"You can grab a couple of slices from mine," Jase offers, already signaling for a waiter. Once everyone has placed their orders, Jase turns his gaze to me. "How are you holding up?"

I scrunch my nose. "I'm okay, just wish I could make things right."

"Give him time."

When Jase just stares at me, I say, "You must be angry with me as well."

He shakes his head lightly. "I'm not happy about what happened, but this thing is between you and Hunter, and it's a mess you'll have to clean up."

"And I will," I promise. "But for what it's worth, I am really sorry."

The corner of Jase's mouth curves up, but there's no warmth on his face. "I'm not the one you wronged, Jade."

I nod, hating that things are awkward between Jase and myself, but I don't blame him. I guess I can thank my lucky stars Fallon and Hana aren't upset with me.

I glance at Mila, and she gives me an encouraging smile. "We should do facials tonight. Just relax."

"Sounds good to me." Under the table, I reach for her hand and give it a grateful squeeze.

"Yeah, I'd pay good money to have you do a facial for me," Jase teases her.

Mila rolls her eyes at him in response. "In your wildest dreams."

"Oh, baby." Jase draws his bottom lip in between his teeth as he stares at Mila. Letting go of it, he murmurs, "You don't want to know what I do to you in my wildest dreams."

I let out a snort and quickly cover my mouth, so I don't burst out laughing. Even I have to admit Jase was hot as fuck, but the stunned look on Mila's face is absolutely priceless.

Chapter 14

HUNTER

As the days go by, I begin to feel a little better. Jade's kept her distance, doing her best to avoid me, and it's given me time to get my emotions under control.

Crossing the lawn between the lecture halls and the restaurant, Jase says, "I'm itching for a night out. We should go to Studio 9 and get wasted."

"Why?" I let my eyes scan over his face, searching for any sign that he might be stressed. "You okay?"

"Yeah." He gives me a playful grin. "Do I need an excuse to get drunk?"

"I guess not," I chuckle. My eyes drift over my surroundings until I spot Jade. She's just come out of the dorm and heading towards the road. Staring at her phone, she seems oblivious to the world around her. From the tightfitting outfit she has on, I guess she's either on her way to the gym or going for a run down one of the trails.

Come to think of it, I haven't seen her at the gym during my morning workouts. She must've changed her time so she won't bump into me.

Jase lets out a low whistle, and hollers, "Looking hot, Jade."

She doesn't respond, her eyes still glued to her phone and it's then I notice the earphones. "She can't hear you."

Without looking up, she begins to cross the road, and the blaring noise from an oncoming car doesn't even get her attention. My heart explodes in my chest, and I rush toward her. My eyes dart between the vehicle that's hitting breaks, and Jade, who just stepped in front of it. Grabbing hold of her arm, I yank her against me and wrapping my arms tightly around her, I swing us to the side of the curb, while my heart races into overdrive.

With Jade's back pinned to my chest, I can't make my arms loosen their grip on her trembling body.

Fuck, that was close.

My breaths explode over my lips from the sudden fright.

"Holy shit," Jade whispers. With a trembling hand, she reaches up and removes the earphones, then says, "Thank you. Shit. I didn't see the car."

Holding her body close to mine wakes my protective streak, and mixing with the fright I just had, it bleeds into anger.

"What the fuck were you thinking?" I snap. Part of me wants to scoop her up and carry her back to the suite where she'll be safe, but my rage wins out, and I finally manage to loosen my grip on her. Grabbing hold of her shoulders, I spin her around and pin her with a glare. "Do you have a death wish?"

Her eyes are wide on my face as she whispers, "I'm sorry, Hunter."

Letting out a chuckle, I shake my head at her. "Those words come easy for you, don't they?" Shoving past her, I bark, "Watch where you're fucking walking. Your so-called accidents are annoying as fuck."

Jase jogs to catch up to me, and I can feel he wants to say something, but he's trying to hold it back. "Spit it out, Jase."

"You don't think that was a little harsh?"

Stopping dead in my tracks, I lock eyes with him, "No, if I hadn't pulled her out of the way, she'd be in an ambulance right now."

"I get you're upset, but she didn't do it on purpose, Hunter," he defends Jade.

I let out a frustrated huff because I know Jase is right. It's just… for a moment back there, I was scared out of my fucking mind, and it let me forget everything Jade has done to me. It reminded me of how much I care about her.

And… for a split-second, having her body pressed against mine made me remember what it felt like when I kissed her.

"Sorry," I apologize to Jase. "I just need a drink."

"See," Jase begins to grin, "we need a night out."

"Yeah, fine," I agree. Getting hammered might help me relax a little.

———————

Jase wasn't joking when he said he wanted to get wasted. Sitting at our regular table at Studio 9, I'm struggling to keep up with him as he downs one whiskey after the other.

"What's the rush?" I ask when he orders two more tumblers.

"I want to get to the fun part as quick as possible," he grins, finishing the last of the whiskey in front of him.

"At this rate, we'll either pass out or puke. Slow down."

His eyes dart past me, and the grin on his face widens. "Finally, the girls are here."

I glance over my shoulder and smile at Fallon and Hana, but then my expression freezes when I see the dress Jade's wearing. The piece of silver fabric hardly covers her ass. My eyes drop to the black knee-high boots that complete her revealing outfit.

"What the hell are you wearing, Jade?" Jase asks the question I've been thinking.

"A dress Fallon dared me to wear. I'm already self-conscious about my butt hanging out for everyone to see. Please, don't make me feel worse," Jade complains as she comes to stand by the table. She drops her little bag, which can't store much more than her phone and a credit card, and says, "I'm going to go dance."

Without looking at me, she makes her way back to the stairs to head down to the dance floor.

Turning my gaze to Fallon, I give her a what-the-hell look. "Why did you let her dress like that?"

Fallon picks up my tumbler and sniffs at it. Pulling a disgusted face, she puts it back down. "God only knows how you drink that stuff." She signals for a waiter and orders a coke before she tilts her head at me, giving me a knowing smile. "Jade has a killer pair of legs and a butt I'd kill for. She should show off her goods with pride. Why do you have a problem with it?"

Letting out a chuckle, I smirk at Fallon, not falling for her bait. "I couldn't care less."

"Why aren't you wearing a sexy number?" Jase asks Mila even though his eyes are roving hungrily over her tight jeans.

"What's wrong with what I'm wearing?" she asks, glancing down at her outfit.

"It's covering too much," Jase teases her.

"Pervert." Mila walks away to join Jade, and I quickly move two chairs up, so I have a clear view of the floor below.

I just want to make sure the girls are okay while they're on the dance floor.

I let out a huff of air and shake my head at myself. Who the fuck am I trying to kid? I'm sitting here like an ass because I know Jade looks fucking hot, and every guy with a working dick is going to notice her.

I might still be angry at her, but it doesn't mean that I don't care.

I down the whiskey a waiter just brought, and feeling lightheaded from the alcohol, I know I should slow down. Still, it doesn't stop me from ordering another glass.

My eyes are glued to Jade as one song blends into another. Another two drinks later, there's a bitter taste in my mouth from all the whiskey, and I'm grinding my teeth.

Carefree, Jade thrusts her hands in the air, and she begins to jump up and down when a fresh beat pulses through the club. Lifting her eyes to the top floor, our gazes collide.

I swear I can feel a spark even though there's a distance between us.

Then Mila throws her head back and laughs as she turns in a circle before swaying to the beat, and it draws Jade's attention away from me.

"Jase, you're missing one hell of a show from Mila," I manage to say without taking my eyes off the girls.

He bumps into me as he comes to sit closer and then lets out a groan. "Damn, she's going to kill me one of these days. Death by blue balls."

I let out a bark of laughter that fizzles away when some guy, who must have a death wish, sidles up behind Jade. He takes hold of her hips, and when his pelvis is practically glued to her ass, I shoot up from my chair.

"I'm coming too," Jase hollers, almost tripping over my chair in his hurry to get up.

I race down the stairs, and as I stalk toward Jade, she pulls an awkward face at Mila, then her gaze sweeps through the dancing throng of people around her until they still on me.

Reaching Jade, I take hold of her arm and pull her against me, and with my right hand, I shove the guy backward and growl, "Get away from her."

"Sorry, I thought she was fair game," he slurs.

Fair game?

Keeping my hold on Jade, I pull back my right arm and let my first connect with the fucker's jaw. He staggers back a couple of steps, and when Jase comes to stand next to me, the guy quickly skulks back into the crowd.

Knowing Mila is safe with Jase, I turn around and pull Jade after me. I'm done watching her dance half-naked while drunk fuckers grind their limp dicks against her ass.

I drag her right out of the club and toward my car.

"Are you guys leaving already?" Kao asks, grabbing my attention. He and Noah must've just gotten here.

"Yeah. Keep an eye on Fallon and Hana. I left them at our table," I bite the words out because I have zero chill right now.

"Drive safely," Kao calls after us.

Jade has been surprisingly quiet, but as I dig my car keys out of my pocket, she says, "I think I should drive. You've had a lot to drink tonight."

I'm not going to argue with her about that, but I can't resist taunting her. "Yeah, and how would you know?" Tilting my head, my voice drops low, "Have you been watching me, Jade?"

"Just give me the keys. We can talk at home." There's no sign of her ever-present fire and spark, and it grinds against my last nerve.

I shove the car keys into her outstretched hand and stalk around the car to the passenger side.

After Jade slides in behind the wheel, she stretches her body over mine, which instantly makes every single one of my muscles tighten. "Just helping with your seat belt," she whispers as she straps me in.

I'm clenching my jaw so damn hard, I won't be surprised if I crack a tooth.

Jade starts the engine, and the vehicle roars to life. My heartbeat is still erratic and just as out of control as my emotions as she drives us back to the dorms.

Where I get the strength from to not lay into her, God only knows.

She's hardly brought the car to a standstill outside of our building when I shove the door open and climb out. The anger that's been simmering on the way home begins to bubble back to the surface. Grabbing her hand, I drag her toward the elevator, and once we're in the confined space, I glare at her.

"I think we should wait to talk until you've sobered up," she says cautiously.

Shaking my head, I say, "No, it's happening tonight."

The elevator doors slide open, and Jade follows me to the front door. Once we're both inside, I slam the thing shut behind us and turn my thunderous gaze on her. "Did you enjoy wearing next to nothing tonight?"

"Huh?" Her expression instantly turns to confusion.

Angrily, I gesture over the length of her body. "That fucking dress can't even be compared to a t-shirt!"

Jade frowns at me, her expression clearly stating she thinks I've lost my mind. "Did you lose your shit because of my outfit?"

"It was either that or have every fucking guy in the club rubbing up against you," I bark.

"Seriously?" There's a spark of anger in her dark eyes. "So, you didn't drag me out of the club so we could finally talk about what happened over the past two years?"

"That's a whole different story," I snap, growing frustrated that she didn't even realize how provocative her outfit looked. "Dressed like that, you might as well go stand on the nearest corner."

Her lips part, and anger ripples over her face. Her features tighten, and it makes her only look sexy as fuck. "You did not just call me a hooker?" she hisses.

Crossing my arms over my chest, I glance over her body. The sight of her tight curves and totally fuckable ass, only makes my anger explode out of control. "Yeah, you totally look the part."

"This is ridiculous!" she snaps, and then my eyes widen as she reaches for the zipper on her side. She pulls it down and shoves the fabric from her shoulders. Watching her wiggle out of the dress, my mouth goes dryer than a desert, and it grows scorchingly hot in the suite.

With Jade standing in her bra, panties, and boots, I have to blink a couple of times, while all my rampant emotions are drowned out by desire.

Fuck, she's looks nothing short of erotic.

"There." She scowls at me. "The dress is gone. Can we talk now?"

My eyes travel back up her body, drinking in the perfect curve of her hips and the taunting V between her legs. Her toned stomach and the firm curve of her breasts peeking from her bra does nothing to quench the heat spreading through me.

When my eyes finally lock on Jade's, I have zero self-control left and darting forward, I bring my hands to her face, and my mouth crashes against hers.

All my frustration, anger, and exhaustion spills over into the kiss, and when Jade tries to push me away, it only spurs me on.

Wrapping an arm around her waist, I yank her body against mine. When her struggle against me intensifies, and she tries to break the kiss, I move my other hand to the back of her neck to keep her in place.

She manages to free her mouth for a moment and cries, "Hunter, stop!"

I'm beyond the point of rationality. My body moves forward, and my touch is biting when I take hold of Jade's neck, crushing her lips beneath mine.

She lets out a whimpering cry and fighting against me to turn her head away, she manages to scream, "Stop!" The flat of her hand connects with the side of my neck, and the sting causes me to flinch away from her.

My eyes focus on her face, and when I see tears glistening on her cheeks, I sober in an instant.

Her breaths explode over her lips, and there's a panic-stricken look in her wide eyes. "Please... just stop," she begs.

The blow is hard as disgust for my actions begins to smother me.

What the fuck did I do?

Darting forward, I wrap my arms around her, and my voice is hoarse as I say, "Fuck, I'm so sorry. I... I..." There's a lump in my throat that's threatening to choke me. "I'm so fucking sorry, Jade."

Bringing her hands up, she pushes me away again. A sob escapes her, making me feel worse than dog shit.

Using the tips of her fingers, her hand visibly trembles as she wipes the tears from her cheeks.

Needing to do something, I run across the room and grab one of the throw blankets from the sofa. I rush back to Jade and quickly wrap it around her shoulders. Seeing the red imprints, my hands have left on her neck and cheeks makes utter devastation rattle me to my core.

I hurt her.

"Christ," I breathe through my horror. "I'm so sorry."

Her breaths shudder through her, and the paleness of her skin only makes the red imprints stand out more. My voice cracks, "I won't hurt you again. This should never have happened. I'm sorry."

She tries to nod, but her shoulders shudder from the sobs wracking through her.

We're destroying each other. This has to stop.

Slowly lifting my hand, I brush the tips of my fingers over the redness on her neck. "Do you need some time, or can we talk?"

She pulls back from my touch and not looking up at me, she shakes her head. "Not tonight."

With a sinking feeling, I watch her walk away from me. I still can't believe that just happened. I wish Jase was here to beat the shit out of me.

JADE

My world's been tilted on its head. I don't know if I'm coming or going.

I've showered and crawled under my covers, but I'm still so shaken up from what happened. Never in a million years did I think Hunter would hurt me.

Not physically.

His handprints have already started to fade away, but the shock is still rippling through me. There was so much anger in the kiss. For a moment, I was terrified of him.

My bedroom door opens, and I freeze, scared that it might be Hunter.

"I'm going to kill Jase one of these days," Mila complains. Leaving the light off, she crawls under the covers and lets out a huff. "All his flirting is driving me insane. By the way, you forgot your purse at the club. I brought it home for you."

She drops the bag on top of me.

Needing to take my mind of the incident between Hunter and me, I ask, "Yeah? What did he do?" Opening the purse, I take my phone out and feeling for my charger in the dark, I plug the device in.

"He practically dry-humped my ass on the dance floor."

A small smile tugs at my lips as I get comfortable again. "Shame, Mila. You should give him a chance."

She lets out a disgruntled huff. "Not in a million years."

"Why?" I ask, snuggling closer to her. Having her here is a soothing balm for me.

"He's a player, and the second I give in, he'll head for the door, and it will be the end of our friendship."

Even though I disagree, I keep it to myself because it's Mila's choice to make. No matter how much I love Jase, I'll never force my friend to do something she doesn't want to.

"Will you sleep here tonight?" I ask, not wanting her to leave.

She turns onto her side. "What happened after you left the club with Hunter? I can't believe he punched that guy. It was insane."

I swallow hard and shake my head. "I don't want to talk about it tonight." I snuggle closer to her and wrap my arm around her waist. "Can you just hug me?"

She wraps me up in a tight hug and presses my face into the crook of her neck. "You can talk to me when you're ready."

We lie in silence, both our minds filled with our problems until sleep finally catches up to us.

When I wake up, I reach out to the bedside table and taking hold of my phone, I squint at it to see what the time is. Seeing I have a message from Hunter, I dart upright and quickly unlock my phone.

Hunter: I'm disgusted with myself. I never wanted to hurt you. I hope you can forgive me. Please listen to

the song because it says everything I want to tell you. Always here. Hunter.

There's a link to Spotify, and I click on it.

Don't Give Up On Me by *Andy Grammar* begins to play, and it makes my emotions burst in my chest. My eyes start to burn, but I blink the tears away, not wanting to miss a second of the song's video.

As much as last night hurt, there's nothing to forgive. Hunter was bound to explode after everything I've put him through.

"I love that song," Mila mumbles from next to me. "We need to watch *Five Feet Apart* again." She peeks up at me then grins sleepily. "We can take a sick day and stay in bed, watching movies and eating junk food."

"That sounds perfect," I say, smiling at her.

She darts out of bed and rushes to the door. "I'm going to get snacks before you change your mind. Sign in to Netflix."

I let out a chuckle, then turn my attention back to my phone.

I scroll through all my playlists, looking for the perfect song to send back to Hunter. Finding one that can speak for how I feel, I share *Surrender*, the *J Breeze* cover with Hunter.

I understand, and there's nothing to forgive. Take all the time you need, and then we can talk things out between us. Never giving up. Jade.

I set my phone down and go to brush my teeth. When my eyes fall on my reflection in the bathroom mirror, I check for any marks. When there are none, I let out a sigh of relief.

I'm going to spend today with Mila and just work through my own emotions before having to face Hunter.

Chapter 15

JADE

I was sure that I could handle seeing Hunter, but the moment I opened my bedroom door and heard his voice from the living room, I slammed the thing shut again.

Yeah, I'm far from ready. I feel anxious, and truth be told, even a little shy, which is an odd emotion. I've never felt self-conscious around any of my friends before.

Yeah, you've also never stripped to your underwear in front of the guys before.

I pull an awkward face and glance around my room, hoping another way out would magically appear.

Damn, I can't miss another day of lectures.

Sucking it up, I press my lips together and open the door again. I keep my eyes on the floor and quickly walk down the hallway, doing my best to not just make a run for the front door.

"She's alive," Jase hollers. "Mila says you watched movies yesterday."

"Yeah, we had an impromptu Netflix day. See ya later," I ramble and rush out of the suite. I quickly jog to the elevator. When I hear the front door open behind me, I make a mad dash for the stairs, not wanting to be caught while waiting for the elevator doors to open.

When I burst through the doors of the dorm, I let out a breath of relief.

I stop by the restaurant and get a cup of coffee from the barista before I head over to my first class.

As the lecture starts, I force myself to pay attention. I take down notes, and when the professor ends the session, I check my schedule to make sure I have ethics next.

I pack up my stuff and file out of the auditorium with the other students, bumping shoulders with the next class already arriving. Making my way down the hallway, I hear Jase's laughter, and my head snaps up, only for my eyes to connect with Hunter's.

"Shit." I begin to back paddle and swinging around, I say, "I… forgot something." I hightail it back to the economics class and fall into the first open seat I can find.

The professor's eyes scan over the students, and I slide down, using my hand to cover my face just in case he recognizes me from the previous lecture.

The group must be third years because I have no freaking clue what the professor is talking about, but my butt remains glued to the seat.

Good one, Jade. Now you're behind in ethics as well.

HUNTER

Jade's avoiding me.

It fucking sucks that she runs away at the sight of me, but I can't blame her.

It's been a long day, and I can't say that I remember anything from my classes.

"This day sucks ass," I grumble to Jase as we walk into the suite.

The one second Jade is standing in the kitchen, and the next, there's no sign of her. I stop by the counter and frown, sure I just saw her drinking a bottle of water.

Jase walks to the fridge and taking two bottles out, he throws one to me, then his eyes go to the floor, a frown forming on his brow.

I watch him lift his chin, and then he grins like an idiot. "Let's go to my room."

I shake my head and walk toward him, which has him widening his eyes at the floor.

Yeah, pretty sure that's where Jade disappeared to.

When I reach the edge of the counter that also serves as a breakfast table, I lean over it and glance down at Jade. "Hey."

Slowly, she glances up, and then she gives me an awkward smile. "H-hey."

When she scrambles up from the floor, I set after her, and before she can shut her bedroom door in my face, I follow her into the room. Locking her only exit, I pocket the key then turn to look at her. "I think it's time we talk. I'm not going to have you hiding just to avoid me."

"I'm not," she blurts out, and when I tilt my head at her, giving her a knowing smile, she begrudgingly admits, "Fine, I'm hiding."

"Is it because you're angry with me. If that's the case, I understand, but I don't want this thing between us getting any worse," I explain.

She quickly shakes her head, and walking to her bed, she slumps down on it. "I'm not angry."

She gives me a quick awkward glance before ducking her head low, then mumbles, "It's because you saw me in my underwear."

I'm surprised by her confession. I was certain she would be angry because I forced a kiss on her. "Let's pretend you were wearing a bathing suit," I offer to make her feel better.

Bullshit, Hunter. No bathing suit on this planet has ever looked so good.

I might have been intoxicated, but I'll never forget the sight of Jade in her bra, panties, and those damn boots.

She gives me a grateful smile, then asks, "Are you really ready to talk, though?"

I walk over to the bed and sit down next to her. "Yeah." Glancing at her, I say, "You start. Tell me why you blamed me."

She clasps her hands together and clears her throat. "I don't have an excuse. I was upset with you for walking in on Brady and me. I think it just got out of hand when I heard he had taken his life." She sucks in a deep breath and lets it out on a sigh. "With time, I convinced myself you had something to do with his suicide. It was stupid of me, and I'm so sorry." Her eyes come up to mine, and I can see the regret written on her face. "I was awful to you, and I'll understand if you can't forgive me, but I'll do anything to make up for it."

There's a moment's silence as I gather my thoughts. "I'm not going to lie, the past two years have been hard." Turning my head to face her, I admit, "You really hurt me."

Her face crumbles a little as if she's fighting not to cry, but she keeps it in. "I'm sorry sounds so inadequate. I wish I could tell you how much I regret my actions."

"I know what you mean," I admit. "My behavior from the other night is right up there with what you did."

Jade shakes her head and stares miserably down at her hands. "Not in a million years, Hunter. Nothing you do can ever compare to the hell I've put you through."

My eyes search over her features. Seeing her remorse is all I wanted. "Where do we go from here?" I ask.

Jade shrugs and whispers, "I have no idea." She shoots me a hopeful glance. "Can't we go back to the way things were?"

I think for a moment, then shake my head. "Too much has changed. I don't think it's possible."

The corners of her mouth pull slightly down, and her chin begins to quiver. "I guess you're right," she whispers as a tear spills down her cheek. "Can we at least make peace and be nice to each other?"

Lifting my hand, I bring it to her face, and with my thumb, I wipe the tear away. I tilt my head to try and catch her eyes, but she keeps staring at her hands. Putting a finger under her chin, I lift her face so she'll look at me. "I'm not saying we can't be friends, Jade. We can take it one day at a time. Let our relationship follow the normal path."

Her face fills with hope, and the corner of her mouth begins to lift in an optimistic smile. "So, you still want to be friends with me?"

"Didn't you listen to the song I sent you this morning?"

"I did," the words burst from her.

"I meant every word. I don't think I can ever give up on us."

"Me too." There's a cute expression on her face. One I haven't seen in years, and it makes me smile. "Are you going to call me Little Bean again?"

I let out a chuckle and shake my head. "You're not so little anymore," I tease her. "It was your childhood nickname, and we both know you're no longer a kid."

Her cheeks flush red, and she buries her flaming face in her hands. Letting out a groan, she complains, "Oh God, I'm never going to live it down." Then her hands drop from her face, and she stares at me with wide eyes. "Please don't tell the others I stripped in front of you."

I can't keep the grin from forming on my face and placing my arm around her shoulders, I pull her into my side. "Your secret is safe with me, but if you ever give me shit again, I'm advertising it to the entire world."

"Deal." She holds her right hand out to me and placing mine in hers, we shake on it.

We sit for a couple of minutes, and I try to think how I'm going to start talking about the topic of the kiss, when Jade says, "About the kiss." Her eyes snap down to her hands, and she shifts awkwardly, which has me dropping my arm from around her shoulders.

"Which one?"

She pulls an uneasy face. "Both, I guess."

I grab onto the most plausible excuse. "We were both just emotional, and at our wits end with each other."

Jade's head instantly bobs up and down. "Totally. You're right."

"We're good?" I ask as I get up.

Jade also rises to her feet. "Ahh… I'm glad we finally made peace, but I still feel like shit. Isn't there anything I can do to make it up to you?"

It's going to take time for our friendship to get back to where it was. I'm just about to tell Jade not to worry about it when an idea pops into my head. "You owe me two years' worth of hugs. You can start by making up for that."

A wide smile splits over her face, and then she face-plants against my chest. When she wraps her arms tightly around my waist, I let out a burst of laughter.

I move my own arms around her and press my mouth to the top of her head. Closing my eyes, I take a deep breath of her scent.

Thank's Jade. This is what I needed. Just being able to hold you again.

I tighten my hold on her, and she responds by snuggling as close to me as she can, and then she whispers, "I'm so sorry. I know you must be tired of hearing me say those words, but I mean them. I'll never forgive myself for the way I treated you."

I still have one question I need to be answered, so I turn my face and resting my cheek against her hair, I ask, "Did you ever stop caring for me?"

"Never." Pulling a little back, she looks up at me. "That's why I was so angry. It felt like I was betraying Brady by still loving you."

I know she means the words as a friend, but they still stir something in my chest. "So, you still love me?" I ask, milking this moment for all it's worth.

Jade breaks free from my arms and quickly pulls her phone from her pocket, then she rambles, "Hold that thought. I have a song for you."

She brings up a playlist, and after pressing play, she holds the phone out for me to take. I look at the screen as she comes to stand next to me, and together we listen to *Sad Song* by *We The Kings*.

The song is so damn cute, and it makes a broad smile form around my lips. I go to place the device on the bed, then turn back to Jade. Taking hold of her waist, I pull her close to me, and when I begin to sway with her, I say, "I owe you a dance."

She lets out a burst of laughter and grins happily up at me. Halfway through the song, she whispers, "Thank you, Hunter."

Giving her a warm smile, I pull her closer, and we dance until the song comes to an end.

Before I pull away from her, she gives me another hug, then teases, "I owe you seven hundred and thirty hugs. I figure if I give you a couple a day, I can pay off my debt faster."

I let out a burst of laughter, and our eyes lock. There's still heartache to work through, but at least we've waved the white flag.

"It's a start," I say to her.

Nodding, she agrees, "It can only get better from here on out."

God, I hope so. More than anything in the world, I want my Jade back.

Chapter 16

JADE

Even though we've made peace, things still feel awkward between us.

You can't expect things to magically go back to the way they were, Jade.

Together we walk out of my room, only to see our friends scatter toward the living room.

"Seeing as you all listened in on our conversation, we don't have to tell you anything," Hunter jokes with them. He makes a beeline for Jase, and slumping down on the couch next to him, he punches Jase's shoulder. "Fucker."

"Oww." Jase rubs his arm. "I wasn't the only one eavesdropping." He lets out a disgruntled huff. "Besides, we couldn't hear shit."

I first go to get myself a bottle of water and take a drink from it. Fallon, Hana, and Mila's eyes keep darting between Hunter and me, and not having the heart to make them suffer any longer, I say, "We've talked things out."

Hana's face instantly lights up. "So, things are good between you again?"

"Yeah." I chuckle when she jumps up, and fist bumps the air.

"Thank God," Jase mutters. "Now, I can focus on my own drama."

Mila's head snaps toward him. "What drama?"

With a heavy sigh, he states, "You giving me a constant case of blue balls."

Mila chokes on air, and the rest of us explode in laughter. When she finally catches her breath, she gives Jase a death glare. "Haha. Always so damn funny."

Jase's face sets into a super serious look. "There's nothing funny about having blue balls. I'm pretty sure it's dangerous. In fact, you could at least give me a handjob and save my life."

Mila drops her forehead into the palm of her hand, shaking her head. "I'm not going to win."

"Nope." Jase lets the P pop. "When you're ready to surrender, just say the word, and we can go to my bedroom."

"Holy shit," she exclaims. "Someone, help me."

"Jase is just fucking with you," Noah says, his shoulders shaking from all the laughing.

"No, I'm not fucking with her," Jase corrects him. "If I were fucking with her, we'd both be in a state of bliss right now." He climbs to his feet and adjusts his crotch as he walks away, looking like he just rode a horse for hours.

We all crack up again, and there's even a smile on Mila's face.

When the fun fades, Fallon says, "Let's order in and watch a movie tonight. I'm too tired to do anything else."

"Sounds like a plan," Hunter agrees.

After thirty minutes of arguing, we end up placing five different orders because we can't decide on just one place to get food from.

"If it was that difficult to order the food, I dread picking the movie," Hana mumbles as she lies down on the couch with her head on Noah's thigh and her legs hanging off the side.

There's a knock at the door, and we all look at it in surprise.

"The food can't possibly be here already," Mila says as she gets up. When she opens the door, she lets out a squeak of surprise. "Oh my gosh! Tristan!" She hugs him before dragging him inside.

Hana's head pops up, and then she falls off the couch in her hurry to get up. "Shit, I'm wearing sweats."

I chuckle as she runs for her room, yelling, "Don't look at me."

Tristan laughs. "You always look beautiful." Then he calls out, "Come back."

"Not a chance in hell. I'll be out in five minutes," she shouts back.

I go to give Tristan a hug. "What's with the surprise visit?"

"I was in the neighborhood and decided to stop by the campus." His eyes keep darting to Hana's closed door.

"So, you and Hana?" I ask, more nosy than anything else.

"Yeah," he takes a deep breath, then asks, "How are things here?"

"Good," I say then catching Hunter's gaze on me, I correct myself, "Actually things are great."

Hunter gives me a warm smile that has my insides doing cartwheels.

It's because you're happy that things are better between you.

Lies, all lies, but I'm not about to admit the truth to myself.

HUNTER

Getting my cardio session in on the treadmill, my eyes scan over the lower floor. Yeah, I'm secretly hoping Jade will start working out in the mornings again.

Just as I slow my pace to cool down, Jade walks into the gym. I watch her look around before she makes her way to the punching bags.

Stepping off the treadmill, I grab my towel and wipe over my face and behind my neck. Pulling my water bottle from the holder, I take a deep drink as I walk toward the stairs.

"Hey, Hunter," some girl greets me on my way down. I just nod my head, my eyes on Jade. She's pulling on a pair of gloves.

Today she's wearing black and purple tight-fitting pants, with a matching top. I still don't like the tight as fuck outfits, but it's gym clothes, so I just have to deal.

Coming up behind her as she jabs at the bag, I can't resist the urge and slap her ass.

"Oh, my God!" she snaps, and spinning around, her arm is already in swinging mode. My hand shoots up, and I block her punch inches from my face. When Jade's eyes focus on me and recognition sets in, she begins to ramble, "Hunter! I'm so sorry. I thought you were some jerk looking for a beating. I didn't mean to almost hit you."

Meaning it as a joke, I say, "Wouldn't be the first time you take a swing at me." I instantly regret my words when a shadow settles over her features. Her lips begin to form the words, but I interrupt her, "Don't apologize, Jade. It's in the past."

"Okay," she murmurs. Then she darts forward and wraps her arms around my waist in a tight hug. "Another one down," she teases as she pulls back, making me grin at her.

Jade's eyes sweep over my body, then she asks, "I didn't see you when I came in, but it looks like you're done with your workout."

"I just finished a cardio session," I explain. "You in the mood to spar?"

Jade tilts her head at me, a smile tugging at her lips. "Do you seriously want to get on the floor with me?"

Get on the floor with me. Those are the only words registering right now as heat sweeps through my body, sending my blood rushing through my veins.

I'd be stone cold and dead not to admit that I find Jade attractive.

Okay, fine, more than attractive.

She's every man's wet dream.

The thought makes me scowl at the students around us to make sure no one is ogling her.

"Yeah." I have to clear my throat when the word sounds like my voice is breaking all over again.

"Okay." Jade gives me a don't cry later look and grabs protective headgear.

I strap on a pair of gloves, and once I have my own headgear on, I move onto a mat. "Show me what you've got, Bean."

A wide grin breaks over her face, and she jumps closer, tapping me on the shoulder with her glove.

I roll my eyes at her. "Come on, don't hold back now."

She takes a swipe at my feet, but I bounce backward, letting out a chuckle. "You're going to have to do better than that."

Like a lightning bolt, she darts forward, and before I know what hit me, my ass is on the floor, and Jade

228

straddles me. She tries to push my arms down on the mat, and I almost fight back, but then I feel her on top of my cock, and I freeze.

It feels like someone took a defibrillator to my heart, shocking the damn thing into overdrive.

Jade wiggles happily on top of me, and yanking my arms from under her hands, I grab hold of her hips to keep her still. "You do not want to wiggle on top of me right now," I warn her.

Jade stills, and her eyes widen. When my words register with her, she darts up so fast that my hands are still hanging in the air where her hips were a moment ago.

"Oh, God," she gasps. She does a weird little dance, then rips the gloves and headgear off. "Ahh…" She does the same awkward two-step, then grabs her towel and water bottle and makes a run for the exit.

Finding her reaction hilarious, I laugh as I climb to my feet. I take off the gear and grabbing my towel and water, I set after her.

I only catch up to Jade when she's in our building, waiting for the elevator to come down from the top floor.

Coming up behind her, I tease, "I have never seen someone move that fast before."

Her head swings to me, and a red flush begins to spread up her neck. "It was an accident," she mutters.

When the doors slide open, she darts into the elevator. I follow behind her and press the button for our floor.

"I'm pretty sure you deliberately dropped my ass to the floor, Jade," I continue to tease her.

"Hunter," she grumbles, glaring down at her feet. "I mean the part where I sat on you."

The doors ping open as I chuckle, "And then wiggled your ass on me."

"Oh, my god. Stop already," she cries as she darts out of the elevator.

When we walk into the suite, I say, "Nope, I'm going to milk this moment for all it's worth."

Jade scowls at me, but before she can say something back, Jase asks, "Did we celebrate the peace between the two of you too soon?"

I grin at him, then say, "Not at all. I'm just giving Jade shit for grinding her ass on me."

"Holy shit," Jade breathes, her face lighting up redder than a ripe tomato.

Jase begins to laugh. "Too much info for me."

I chuckle as she makes a run for her room, and I call out, "Only joking with you, Jade."

"Joking, my ass," Jase mutters. He gives me a knowing look then wags his eyebrows. "So, you and Jade? I never would've guessed that in a zillion years."

"Huh?" I frown at him. "What the hell are you talking about?"

Giving me a satisfied grin, he says, "You'll realize soon enough. Fuck," he opens the front door, and as he leaves, he continues, "I'm going to enjoy this show."

What show? What the fuck is Jase on about?

Shrugging, I go to shower so I won't be late for class.

JADE

Falling face down on my bed, I cover my head with a pillow and scream.

What the hell just happened?

I toss the pillow to the side and turn onto my back. Staring up at the ceiling, I try to make sense of it all.

Hunter was just joking with you, Jade.

Then… why did it feel like he was flirting?

And I'm pretty sure I felt him turning hard beneath my butt. I grab another pillow and shove it over my face.

Oh. My. God. I felt Hunter's cock.

I let out a burst of embarrassed laughter that sounds more like a shriek. Then I dart upright and tilt my head as a thought forms in my head.

Does that mean he's attracted to me?

Or do guys get hard at the drop of a hat?

I have zero experience in *that* department, but knowing there's one person I can ask, I reach across the bed and grab my phone from where it was charging. I bring up Miss Sebastian's number and press dial.

"My god-baby," she croons over the line. "To what do I owe this early call?"

"I just wanted to say hello," I lie.

"Well… hello," she says with a playful tone. "How are things at school?"

"Good." I scrunch my nose and let out a huff. "Mamma G, can I ask you a private question?"

"Of course. What can I help with." I hear something in the background, then Miss Sebastian snaps, "Not now, my chunk of hunk. I'm on the phone."

I grin when I hear her husband ask, "Who are you talking to?"

"Jade. She needs advice. Now skedaddle your bedazzled ass out of the room. Us girls need our privacy." A couple of seconds later, she says, "Talk to me, my god-baby."

"Well… ahh… first promise you won't tell my dad." I widen my eyes as I wait for her reply.

"I promise unless you're doing drugs, then all bets are off, and even I will tan your bedazzled behind with my diamond-studded belt."

"No drugs," I assure her quickly, then covering my eyes with my free hand, I ask, "Uhm… do guys get hard… ah… down there… for just any reason?" There's no way I can use the word cock with Miss Sebastian. She's my godmother for crying out loud.

"Say what now," she asks, sounding dumbstruck. "Like a hard-on?"

"Uh-huh." I pinch my eyes shut and pull an awkward face. "Sorry for asking you, but I was curious and have no one else to ask."

"It's fine, my god-baby. You can come to me with anything. Okay, time to get serious." She takes a deep breath, then continues, "A cock only gets hard if it sees something it likes."

I burst out laughing because this is getting embarrassing. I never thought I'd have a conversation like this with my godmother. "Oh… my… god."

"Why are you laughing?"

"You said the C-word," I admit, my voice thick with laughter.

"Cock?" she asks, chuckling.

"Yeah, that one."

"Come on, you can say it." She waits, and when I remain silent, she says, "Cock. Cock. Cock. Maybe if I say it enough, you won't be so uncomfortable with it anymore."

"Stop," I cry with another burst of laughter. "You're my godmother. I'm not saying it in front of you."

"Cock. Cock. Cock." Suddenly Miss Sebastian screeches in my ear, "Not yours, Ryan! Get out."

Tears begin to stream down my face, and I gasp for air.

When I finally calm down, Miss Sebastian asks, "Did some guy get handsy with you? Do I need to come over there and kick some ass with my bedazzled heels?"

"No, not at all," I quickly put her at ease. "I was just wondering how that part of the body worked."

"Cock. Say it," she orders.

"C-c-ooooh," I begin to chuckle then spit the word out. "Cock."

"Awww… I'm so proud of my god-baby, saying cock for the first time," Miss Sebastian croons.

"Uh-huh," I respond. "I'm sure it's every godparent's dream."

"Honestly, I'd rather have you talk to me about these things than hide it from me." Miss Sebastian clears her throat, then she asks, "Are we talking about a boy you like?"

Her question catches me off guard, and the smile fades from my face. "I don't know," I whisper, then I admit. "I care a lot about him, but I'm not sure whether we're friends or something else."

"How do you feel when you're around him?" she asks another straightforward question.

I think it over, then answer, "We used to fight a lot, but then things started changing, and after we made peace, everything's been awkward between us."

"Oooh… nothing like a good enemies to lovers romance," she states. "By the way, are we talking about Hunter Chargill?"

My eyes widen, and I gasp, "How did you know?"

"Babygirl, everyone knows the two of you have been fighting like cats and dogs," she admits.

"Even my parents?" I ask, wondering what gave it away.

"Yep, your daddy knows. The scathing looks you gave each other were a dead giveaway."

"Crap," I breathe.

"You didn't answer my question, though. Are we talking about Hunter?"

"Yeah." My shoulders drop because I don't know what to make of the mess in my heart.

"Wanna tell me what happened?" Miss Sebastian asks.

"I found out he wasn't responsible for Brady committing suicide, and now I feel like dog poop because I fought with him for two years. We talked about it and waved the white flag, but since then, I don't know what to feel."

"It's only natural, baby girl," Miss Sebastian tries to offer me some comfort. "I suppose you can't go back to the way things were before the fighting started?"

"No, we both changed a lot over the past two years. I think the gap is too big," I answer, sounding almost pitiful because I'm at such a loss at what to do.

"Okay, first things first. You do still care for Hunter, right?"

"Yeah, I never stopped." I lie back on my bed and stare up at the ceiling.

"And judging by the reason for this call, there might be more than just friendly feelings involved?" she asks.

I'm quiet for a moment, thinking over her question, then I whisper, "Honestly… yeah, I think I'm attracted to Hunter." Reaching off the bed, I grab the pillow I tossed on the floor earlier. Laying back down, I shove it over my face and mumble, "He's an amazing person, and I think I'm falling for him."

"What's that? I can't hear shit if you mumble," she complains.

Lifting the pillow, I say louder, "I think I'm falling for him."

My door swings open, and Kao's head pops in. "Who are you falling for?"

"God! Get out!" I throw the pillow at Kao just as Hunter comes out of his own room, asking, "Who's falling for who?"

Scrambling over the side of my bed, I drop to the floor so I can hide behind it while my face practically goes up in flames. "Crap, he heard," I whisper to Miss Sebastian.

"Kao won't snitch on you," she says. "Tell my god-baby I say hi."

I peek over the bed as Kao tosses the pillow back at me. "You're going to be late for class."

"Mamma G says hi. Close the door." I duck back down, wishing the ground will open beneath me. "I think Hunter heard the part about me falling for him," I continue to whisper.

"It's not like you said his name," Miss Sebastian states.

"Oh, right," I breathe a sigh of relief.

"Okay, so just to make sure I'm on the right page of this story, are you in love with Hunter?"

I let out a winning sound. "I don't know. It might be that I'm just feeling regret for my actions."

"Honey, there's a huge difference between being in love and feeling regret. Do you get butterflies around him?"

I think over the question. "It sometimes feels like my insides are doing cartwheels," I admit.

"Same thing," Miss Sebastian says. "Do you know how he feels about you?"

Frowning, I pull a face at the phone, then bring it back to my ear. "Mamma G, he probably still hates me."

"Yeah, with a hard dick," she says drily.

Widening my eyes, I cry, "Noooooooo."

"Oh, yes," she chuckles. "Listen, baby girl, your vajayjay gets tingles, and his ding-dong gets hard. That's how it all starts."

I cover my mouth, then my eyes, then drop my hand back to my mouth as I make a choking sound.

"And it's all okay," Miss Sebastian continues as if she didn't just embarrass the hell out of me. "You should be enjoying it. Oh, to be young and in love."

In love? Is this really what I'm feeling?

"I guess," I reply.

"Don't worry about it, baby girl. But before you enjoy the ride, make sure you're on the pill," she warns.

"I'm just going to disappear into the ground now," I complain, but then assure her anyway, "I'm on the pill."

"Oh good," she sighs relieved, then adds, "Make sure Hunter's wrapped in a raincoat before he brings his cock anywhere near you."

I let out another choking sound that morphs into a whine. "Stop already. I'm dying here."

There's a moment's silence, then Miss Sebastian says, "All laughs aside. Just go with your heart, Jade, and I'm here if you're ever in doubt."

"I love you, Mamma G."

"Love you more than anything in the world," she says. "I have to run. My chunk of hunk hasn't had breakfast yet, and he's probably prowling a ditch in the floor outside the bedroom door."

"Yeah, go… uhm… feed him," I say awkwardly.

"Get your mind out of the gutter," she snaps, then with a chuckle, she explains, "I'm talking about actual food."

I begin to laugh. "My bad. Thanks for listening to me."

"Always."

I drop the phone and lie down on the floor, closing my eyes.

Well, that conversation just happened.

Chapter 17

HUNTER

Since I overhead Kao and Jade, the words have been playing on a non-stop loop in my mind.

Who are you falling for?

Is she in love with someone?

There's a sinking feeling in my gut that has me coming to a sudden halt on the pavement.

"Why are you stopping?" Jase asks, glancing around us to see what got my attention.

Turning my head to Kao, I ask, "Is Jade in love with someone?"

"Fuck if I know," he shrugs. "I just overheard her yelling *I'm falling for him* as I was passing by her room."

"For real?" Noah asks.

Jase lets out a chuckle. "Well, I'm not surprised."

All three of our heads snap toward Jase. "What do you know that we don't?" Kao asks the question I'm thinking.

Jase just shrugs.

Noah pats him on the shoulder then gestures toward the lecture halls. "See you later. Kao and I have to get to class."

Jase and I watch them walk away, then he turns a grin to me and wags his eyebrows.

"Is that code for something?" I ask as I begin to walk again. Our lecture is at nine, so we're on our way to grab some breakfast.

We begin to walk again, and Jase just keeps grinning like an idiot.

"Seriously, what do you know?" I ask, frustration sharpening my words.

He shrugs again. "I'm just glad I won't be the only one walking around with blue balls."

"What the hell are you talking about?"

We enter the restaurant and go to our usual table. Sitting down, I stare at Jase until he says, "You and Jade."

"What about us?" Letting out a sigh, I ask, "Are we even having the same conversation?"

We give our orders to the waiter before Jase answers, "Now that you're done fighting, y'all are hot for each other."

"Huh?" I blink at him like an idiot.

Jase rests his elbows on the table, leaning closer to me. "You were teasing her this morning about sitting on your lap."

"So?" Fuck, I'm lost.

He sucks in a deep breath and glances up as if he's running out of patience. "Dude, you were flirting with Jade."

The expression on my face goes blank, and all I can do is stare at Jase.

I was?

Fuck, I was.

"I think Jade was talking about you," Jase continues with his sudden burst of wisdom. "Think about it. You flirted with her, and she made a run for her room. She probably called someone to talk to, seeing as you confused the fuck out of her."

Christ. I so did not see this coming.

I rub a hand over my face and let out a sigh. "You really think she was talking about me?"

"Yep, after that hot kiss at the club, there's no doubt in my mind," he states.

A waiter brings our coffee, and I watch as Jase drinks his. He doesn't know about the second kiss.

"I kissed her again," I admit.

Jase chokes and spews coffee over the whole damn table. I dart back, almost falling over in my hurry to get away from the flying liquid.

A server rushes to our table and begins to wipe up the mess.

"What happened here?" Fallon asks, having just entered the restaurant.

My head snaps up. "Jase spat his coffee everywhere."

"His fault," Jase croaks before he coughs.

Fallon and Hana sit down, and Hana asks, "What did you do?"

"Me?" I give them an innocent look. "Nothing."

"Bullshit," Jase coughs. Pointing his finger at me, he says, "Hunter was just about to tell me about his second kiss with Jade."

"What?" both the girls gasp. Fallon scoots closer to me, "When did this happen? Tell us everything!"

I let out a chuckle, but it quickly fades when I think of the disastrous kiss. "It... I... I fucked up."

All three of their faces instantly sober up, and they all stare at me until I admit, "It was the night I got a little drunk at Studio 9." I drop my eyes to the table. "We got into another fight, and then I lost my shit and kissed Jade."

When I only get silence, I glance up. They're just staring at me, waiting for more. "I forced the kiss on Jade."

Fallon's the first to react. She darts in my direction and slaps me upside the head, and then Jase follows up with punching the shit out of my shoulder.

But my eyes go to Hana, and when she drops her eyes from mine, and a sad look settles on her face, I feel like dog shit all over again.

"I didn't mean for it to happen," I try to explain.

Hana just nods, not looking at me. She begins to get up, which has me darting out of my chair. I grab hold of her arm before she can walk away.

It's grown quiet in the restaurant, and I know everyone can hear our conversation when I say, "Don't walk away. Please. Let me explain."

Hana lets out a sigh and glancing at me with a trembling chin, she gives in and goes to sit down again. I take the chair next to hers and pull her into a hug. "I'm sorry, Hana. I had too much to drink that night, and I know it's no excuse. I feel like shit."

"It doesn't matter how you feel," she mutters. When her eyes meet mine, there's a world of pain in them I didn't expect to see. "It only matters how you made Jade feel. She was supposed to be safe with you, and she wasn't."

My heart begins to beat harder. "I get a feeling we're not talking about Jade and me."

Hana quickly drops her gaze from mine and whispers, "We are talking about you."

Anger ripples over my body, and breathing speeds up. "What happened, Hana?"

She keeps staring down, and then her eyes drift close. The distraught look on her face knocks the air from my lungs.

Jase's eyes are glued to Hana, worry darkening his features.

Fallon wraps an arm around Hana's shoulders, and pressing her head to Hana's, she whispers, "Did something happen?"

Hana just nods.

I'm going to kill someone.

"Tell us," Jase demands, his voice as dark as the emotions wreaking hell inside of me.

"I can't." Hana looks up at us, a pleading look on her face. "I'm dealing with it. Things are just hard right now."

"Did something happen with Tristan?" Fallon asks.

Hana quickly shakes her head. "No! No, he has nothing to do with this. You can't tell him anything."

"Did someone hurt you?" Jase asks, still on the warpath.

"No." Hana shakes her head, then lets out a miserable sigh. "Forget about it, please." She brings her eyes to me. "Did you apologize to Jade?"

Deciding to back down for now and to not push Hana to open up, I nod. "We made peace after it."

"At least something good came from it." Hana tries to smile, but it doesn't reach her eyes.

I pull her to my chest and giving her a hug, I whisper, "I'm here whenever you need to talk. But please tell me if someone is hurting you."

"No one's hurting me," she murmurs against my ear. I just got upset on Jade's behalf."

I know she's lying to me, and it's something I'm not used to. The four of us don't keep any secrets from each other.

Suddenly Jase shouts, "The show is fucking over, everyone! Fucking nosy fuckers."

It's seldom Jase gets angry, but when he does, it might as well be pouring fire and fucking brimstone.

"Why are you yelling?" Mila suddenly asks.

Jase gets up and giving her a dark scowl, he snaps, "Fuck, not you, too."

"What did I do?" she gives him a shocked look.

Knowing things are about to get totally out of control, I dart up and wrapping my arm around Jase's shoulders, I drag him out of the restaurant.

"Calm down," I whisper as I steer him toward the trail behind the restaurant, so we'll have privacy.

He shoves me away from him, and then his angry gaze burns on me. "Hold up." Tilting his head, he asks, "You forced yourself on Jade?"

Oh. Fuck.

I'm about to get that beating I begged for after it happened. Not about to shy away from the mistake I made, I nod.

Jase's punch to the corner of my mouth makes me stagger backward, but before I lose my balance, he grabs hold of my arm and pulls me into a hug.

Our breaths rushing mixes with the birds chirping around us for a couple of seconds, then Jase whispers, "Don't ever do that to Jade again."

I nod, actually feeling a bit better because I deserved the punch and so much more.

When we pull free from the hug, I ask, "So we're good?"

Jase grins, and the sight chases away the last of the lingering worry. "We're good."

"Wanna take a walk?" I ask.

"Yeah."

Shoving our hands in our pockets, we stroll down the path.

"Do you think someone hurt Hana?" Jase asks.

I shrug, not sure. "She said no one hurt her. Maybe she just got into a fight with someone?"

Jase lets out a sigh of relief. "Yeah, you're probably right." He chuckles, "I was scared there for a moment."

"Me too."

He bumps his shoulder against mine. "Getting back to our discussion before the shit hit the fan…" Glancing at me with a smirk, he continues, "So you and Jade, huh?"

I shake my head and let out a heavy breath. "I have no idea what's going on between us. For the longest time, all we did was fight, and now that there's nothing to fight about, things are awkward. It's like we don't know how to communicate with each other."

Jase makes kissing sounds, puckering his lips at me.

Shoving him away from me, I chuckle. "Stop your shit."

Jase comes to stand next to me again, and we stare out over the landscape.

"Okay, I'm serious now," he says. Giving me a somber look, he places his hand on my shoulder. "I know it's been a while since you've gotten laid, so just remember to stick her with the pointy end."

Laughter bursts from me. "You're quoting Game of Thrones to me right now?" I shove him away again. "Fucker."

He throws his arm around my shoulders and smiles at me. "Whether you and Jade just remain friends, or decide there's more, I'll be here rooting for you."

He keeps bringing it up, and it has me asking, "You really think there's more between us?"

Nodding, he lets out a sigh. "The tension is there, like a huge-ass elephant, you can't help but notice."

"What tension?" I ask, and when he grins at me, I already regret the question.

"The good kind." Turning his gaze back to the landscape in front of us, he continues, "The kind that leads to mindblowing orgasms."

I can only shake my head at him, and as we stand, each drawn into our own thoughts, one stands out for me — *Are Jade and I falling for each other?*

Chapter 18

JADE

When my last lecture for the day ends and I get back to the suite, the girls decide to spend the rest of our Friday afternoon doing facials and just chilling.

Hana brings the skin products and masks to the living room, while Fallon and I grab some drinks and snacks. Mila switches on the TV and gets the movie ready we'll be watching during our pamper and pig out session.

"What movie are you putting on?" Fallon asks Mila as she dumps candy into a bowl.

"Midnight Sun. Are you okay with that one?"

"Oooh… I love it," I reply, picking up the tray of cokes, and carrying over to the table. Sitting down on the ground, I add, "We should watch The Fault In Our Stars after that one."

"Yeah, I'm in need of a good ugly cry," Hana says as she plops down on the carpet next to me.

"Why?" I ask, my eyes searching her face.

"Ugh, it's nothing," she sighs. "Tristan's just under a lot of pressure with a business deal he's working on."

"Is that all?" Fallon asks as she places the bowls of candy next to the cokes.

"Yeah."

Mila and I just stare at them, then Hana says, "I blew my top at Hunter earlier today and got them worried over nothing."

"Why did you get angry with Hunter?" Mila asks.

Hana gives me a regretful smile. "Because he forced a kiss on Jade."

My mouth drops open on a gasp. "He told you?"

"It just kinda came out," Fallon quickly stands up for him. "But seriously, it's not cool, and I hate that you didn't tell us, and I still want to kick Hunter's ass."

"It was nothing," I mumble, and not wanting Hunter to get shit from Fallon and Hana, I explain, "It's actually my fault because I stripped in front of him."

"You did what?" Fallon asks, her eyes widening.

My shoulders slump, and I let out a huff of air. "Hunter was all angry about the dress you had me wear to the club, and I lost my shit and stripped out of it. He then totally lost it, and that's when the kiss happened. But he regretted it instantly, and I'm okay, so it's all settled."

My eyes dart between my friends as I pull an awkward face.

Hana grins at me. "I can actually picture you ripping the dress off. It's so like you."

"And totally explains why Hunter kissed you," Fallon agrees.

"Hold up," Mila says, throwing a hand in the air. "Did I miss something? Are you and Hunter a couple now?"

I let out a burst of laughter. "No!"

She throws both her hands in the air. "Well, shit, then I'm lost."

Fallon looks to Mila and scoots closer to the table. "They kissed twice, but they're still in denial."

"That's for sure," Hana sighs before she pops an M&M in her mouth.

"We aren't in denial," I huff.

"Yeah?" Fallon says, lifting an eyebrow at me. "You sure about that?"

Am I?

I let out a miserable sigh. "No."

"I swear, this is just getting more confusing by the minute," Mila grumbles. Pinning me with her eyes, she asks, "Do you and Hunter like each other?"

"Of course, we like each other." I frown at her. "At least I like him. I'm not so sure where he stands after all the fighting."

"No! Ugh," Mila scowls at me. "Are you in love?"

"Oh… ahh…" My mouth snaps shut, and I shrug, not knowing what to answer.

Mila relaxes, and a smile spreads over her face. "Finally, I know what's going on as well."

"People don't just fall in love," I grumble. "That shit takes time."

Fallon shakes her head at me. "I'm afraid not. It usually slaps you upside the head. It's staying in love that takes time and effort."

"Nah… we just like each other as friends," I try to stop this conversation from derailing.

"Picture Hunter dressed in just his sweatpants, all sweaty and muscles hard," Mila says, her voice low.

"Ewww," Hana pulls a traumatized face where Fallon instantly starts shaking her head.

Me, on the other hand, lights up like a damn Christmas tree. The thought of Hunter's bare chest on full display sends a burst of heat ricocheting through my body like fireworks.

As the realization settles in my heart, I cover my face with my hands and let out a groan.

Shit, somewhere… somehow… I've fallen in love with Hunter.

"How did it happen?" I groan out in misery.

"How did it not happen sooner?" Mila counters my question. I drop my hands and push my bottom lip out, giving her my most pitiful facial expression, but she continues, "Hunter put up with your shit for two years. Honestly, he's a damn saint if you ask me."

Fallon nods in agreement.

I just have to face the truth. "Yeah, Hunter's an amazing person," I admit.

"And?" Hana spurs me on to continue.

"And…" A smile pulls at the corner of my mouth, "Isn't it weird that I've fallen in love with him? We've been friends since forever."

"Love is love," Fallon gives her opinion. "You can't choose who you're going to love, Jade. You can only hope the person will love you back."

"Yeah. That will never happen." I pick up a glass of coke and take a huge sip.

"Don't be too sure of that," Hana murmurs as she begins to hand out the facial masks.

"What do you mean?" I ask as I tear mine open.

While I struggle to keep the wet fabric from twisting into a mess, Hana answers, "Hunter doesn't go around just kissing girls."

"What she said," Fallon confirms as she splats her mask onto her face.

Hana chuckles and climbing to her knees, she reaches over to help Fallon straighten the mask out over her skin.

Hunter doesn't go around just kissing girls.

And he's kissed me twice. My eyes dart to Mila's, and she gives me an encouraging smile. "If you love Hunter, then just go for it, Jade."

"Yep," Fallon mutters so she won't wrinkle the mask.

I slide my own mask on and point to the TV. "Press play."

As the movie starts, my thoughts are consumed with Hunter, and what the new emotions creeping into my heart means.

"Don't forget, tomorrow is the fun day," Hana says. "Jase will be at the kissing booth, so make sure to stop by there."

"I totally forgot," I admit. "A fun day is just what I need."

"It starts at eight," Fallon reminds me. "And wear a bathing suit under your clothes because we'll probably play some volleyball in the pool."

"Awesome." I turn my gaze back to the TV, and we all settle in to watch the movie.

HUNTER

Standing by the kissing booth, I burst out in laughter when Jase grabs hold of a girl and proceeds to kiss the living hell out of her.

When he lets go of her shoulders, she stumbles backward, totally dazed.

"Slow down, heartbreaker," I call out to him.

"Jase looks like he's having fun," Fallon suddenly says behind me.

Glancing over my shoulder, my eyes connect with Jade's, and a smile instantly spreads over my face.

Fallon comes to stand next to me, glancing over the long line of girls who bought tickets to kiss Jase. "At least Trinity is making a ton of money for charity."

"Yeah," Glancing behind me again, I ask, "Who's doing the three-legged race?"

"I'm doing it with Kao," Fallon answer.

"Noah asked me to be his partner," Hana says before she pops a fry into her mouth.

"I'm with that idiot," Mila grumbles, gesturing at Jase. "When he's done slobbering on all the girls."

"And you?" I ask Jade.

She shakes her head, then coming to stand on my other side, she wraps her arm around my waist and gives me a sideways hug, then she explains, "I totally forgot about the fun day."

"That makes two of us," I admit. When Jade begins to pull away from me, I put my arm around her shoulders and tug her back against my side. "Jase signed me up so you can run with me."

"Cool." She grins up at me, her eyes sparkling.

"I need chapstick," Jessica calls out from behind her booth, yanking my attention away from Jade. "My poor lips."

"I have some," Hana yells back and rushing over to the stage, she gives Jessica the balm.

"What time is the three-legged race?" Jade asks.

"In thirty minutes." Fallon gives the long line a skeptical look, then she glances at me. "Jase will have to take a break for the race and then come back unless you step up to help him."

"Me?" I ask. My eyes dart down to Jade's and then to the line of girls before I glare at Fallon. "Hell no."

"Come on," Fallon keeps going. "Go help Jase out."

Shaking my head, I press my lips tightly together. "Hm-uh."

"You'd make some dreams come true," she teases.

"Don't care," I mutter. "My lips aren't touching some random girl's."

Fallon is just about to say something when Jade places her hand on my abs and leans forward so she can see Fallon. "Stop, already. Hunter said no." I give Jade a thankful smile and wink, which has her grinning at me. "Don't worry. I've got your back."

Fallon smirks at us. "Just making a point."

"What point?" I ask.

"Nothing," Jade snaps, giving Fallon a look of warning. Pulling away from me, she says, "I'm going to get some water before the race."

"Hold up," I call after her. "I'll go with you." Catching up to Jade, we walk to the stands selling drinks. I hand over the dollar bills and grab two bottles for us. Handing Jade one, I ask, "So I guess it means you also didn't sign up for the volleyball later?"

She takes a huge sip, then shakes her head.

"Good, you can be with me for that as well."

Jade's wet lips curve into a smile, and it has me staring like an idiot. All I can think of is how those lips felt against mine.

Yeah, Hunter. No use in pretending you don't have the hots for Jade.

Wanting to know where her mind is at with what happened to Brady, so I don't make a stupid move she's not ready for, I ask, "How are you handling things after Colton's visit?"

Jade gestures toward a tree. "Let's get some shade." When we sit down on the grass, she begins to pick at a blade. "I'm okay. I just hate that I didn't know. I feel guilty for not seeing the signs." She shrugs, a sad look washing over her face.

"It still hurts," I state, wondering if she'll ever get over what happened.

Jade brings her eyes up to mine. "I think a part of me will always grieve for Brady. He deserved so much more than what life gave him."

"Yeah," I agree with her. Stretching my legs out in front of me, I lean back on my elbows and let my eyes glance over the students and all the fun they're having.

"But it's in the past," Jade surprises me by continuing. "It's time for me to start living in the present."

Our eyes lock, and an intense emotion passes between us.

It can't just be me feeling this way, can it?

"The present's a pretty good place to be," I murmur.

"Yeah," she breathes.

Our eyes remain locked until Mila suddenly asks, "Are you having a staring contest?"

We both quickly look away, and I climb to my feet. "Is it time for the race?"

"Yeah, I came to tell you."

Passing the booth, I see Fallon managed to get Nate to take over from Jase. He spots us and calls out, "I hope you buy a ticket, Jade."

"In your dreams, Nate," I yell back, throwing my arm around Jade's shoulders. I yank her to my side, and when she stumbles, her hand splays out across my abs, so she doesn't lose her balance, and she lets out a burst of laughter.

"Mila, how about you?" Nate shouts.

Mila sticks her hand in the air, waving a little slip of paper, and yells, "Got my ticket. See you after the race."

"Give me that ticket," Jase growls, and he yanks it from her hands. Ripping it to shreds, he tosses the scraps in the first available bin. "Hell will freeze over before you kiss Nate fucking Sparks."

"Hey!" Mila shrieks. She darts toward Jase and it has him grinning while he sprints away from her. "Just wait until I get my hands on you! You can't run forever, Jase."

I let out a chuckle as I watch Mila try to catch Jase. He keeps darting away from her.

"You think they'll ever get together?" Jade asks. She wraps her arm around my lower back as we walk towards the stretch of lawn marked off for the race.

"One day," I sigh. "Hopefully."

"Yeah."

When we get to the start line, an attendant ties one of my legs to Jade's with a piece of fabric.

Mila finally gets to slap Jase upside the head as they come to stand next to us.

I glance down at Jade, and when she grins up at me, I wink at her. "We're going to kick ass, right?"

"You bet."

We wait for all the contestants to get ready, and I tighten my grip around Jade's shoulders as we wait for the whistle to blow.

The shrill sound creates chaos as some manage to get away from the starting line while others trip and fall.

Jade and I manage just fine, but when Jase and Mila begin to overtake us, Jase and I try to push each other off balance. Jade's laughter echoes over the field, and her hand grips hold of my shirt over my chest as she struggles to keep running.

Fallon and Kao come out of nowhere and race through the finish line. Kao immediately wraps Fallon in a hug. "Yassss, baby! That's how it's done."

When Jade and I cross the line in second place, I pull her against my chest and press a kiss to the top of her head.

"That was so much fun," she chuckles. When she tilts her head back, and I see the laughter shining from her eyes, everything feels perfect.

Chapter 19

HUNTER

This is easily one of the best days of my life.

When we get to the pool for the volleyball game, I have a permanent grin on my face. But when the girls walk in, only wearing bikini's, the smile quickly fades, and I ask, "Don't any of you own one-piece bathing suits?"

"What's wrong with these?" Fallon asks.

"Skin," I growl, and it draws a chorus of laughter from the girls.

"Come on, we need to get our heads in the game," Mila says. "We can't lose against Nate and Jessica's team."

Grabbing hold of my shirt, I pull it over my head and drop it by our towels. Turning back, I catch Jade staring at me... or rather my chest.

"Eyes on the ball, Jade," I tease her before I dive into the water. Coming up for air, I wipe the drops from my face, and it's in time to watch Jade jump in, sending a spray of water my way.

When her head pops above the water, I wrap an arm around her waist and pull her to the side. "Climb on my shoulders, monkey."

"How?" she asks.

"Hold on." Taking a deep breath, I duck under the water and come up between her legs. I almost swallow water as a thought I should not be thinking right now flashes through my mind.

Dirty and hot.

When I have Jade on my shoulders, I push her into the air as my head breaks through the water.

"Holy crap," Jade shrieks, her arms wide at her sides to keep her balance. "This is so much harder than it looks."

"Just find your balance. We have a minute."

"Right." Her hands alternate from almost yanking my hair out to twirling wildly in the air.

"Hook your feet behind his back," Fallon calls out.

Jade listens and finally manages to find her balance, but it causes a problem for me, seeing as the warmth of her pussy is flush with my neck.

Jade's pussy. Now there's a thought.

"Hunter."

"Hunter!"

"What?" I almost glance up but stop myself in time from throwing Jade off balance.

"The game's about to start."

"Oh, yeah." I move us toward our position.

Jade squirms, shifting closer to me, and it only makes my focus snap from the game to the heat between her legs. I almost go under the water, but catch myself in time.

Oh God. I'm going to drown today.

I'm just glad my lower half is under the water because I'm hard as fuck.

This is going to be one hell of a *hard* game to play.

Pun intended.

Fallon serves the ball, starting the game. I'm fucking impressed with myself when I manage to focus on the ball. Jade stops a shot and wacks it back toward the other team, sending it sailing over their heads.

"Nice goal, babe," I praise her, rubbing my hands over her knees.

Hana leans over to us to high-five Jade.

Thank god the game is only twenty minutes long. When we win with one point, I sink under the water and turning toward Jade, I wrap an arm around her waist before I shoot us up into the air.

Jase and Kao holler in victory while Mila and Fallon do a victory dance in the water.

My eyes turn to Jade, and without thinking, I press a quick kiss to her smiling lips. Pulling back, I try to save face by saying, "Good game."

Lame, Hunter. So fucking lame.

I let go of Jade and swim toward Jase.

JADE

I've been in a daze since Hunter plastered a super quick kiss against my lips.

It doesn't really count as a kiss, Jade.

After all the fun on campus, Jase is begging us to go to the club.

"I'm tired," Fallon whines.

"Me too," Noah adds. "I can fall asleep right where I'm sitting."

I've just showered and changed into a pair of sweatpants and a t-shirt. I sit down on the arm of the couch closest to me and say. "Let's just watch a movie."

Hunter walks by me and gestures to Fallon. "Make space for me." When she moves up, he sits down and then grabs hold of my hips, yanking me onto his lap.

What's happening?

With wide eyes, I stare at Mila, who's across from me. She gives me a reassuring smile and mouths, *'Just go with it.'*

"We can go tomorrow night," Hunter says.

"Fine," Jase relents. "But then we have to play a game."

"What game?" Kao asks. "Your last game sucked. Literally."

Kao's comment makes me remember when Hunter kissed me at the club, and it sends a wave of heat up my neck.

Hunter gives my hip a squeeze, telling me he knows what I'm thinking.

Well, this isn't awkward at all.

Jase shrugs as he pulls his phone from his pocket. "It's either the game or Studio 9."

"Let's play the game," Mila says, drawing a wide grin from Jase. He jogs to the kitchen and grabs a bottle of whiskey and a couple of tumblers.

Hunter chuckles. "Do we have to start worrying about you drinking too much?"

"Come on," Jase says. "It's me we're talking about."

"My point, exactly," Hunter comments drily. I begin to get up, but Hunter tightens his grip on my hip. "Stay."

Ahhh.... Okay, then.

I shift my legs over the side of his thighs and squeeze my butt into the corner, resting my back against the armrest, and I lean my head against his shoulder.

Jase places the phone on the coffee table and pours each of us a shot of whiskey.

When we all have something to drink, Jase presses spin on the phone. The arrow lands on Hana.

What's your darkest secret?

She chuckles and shrugs. "I once stole fifty dollars from my dad's wallet to buy candy."

"That sounds like something my mother would do," Hunter comments.

"That's a lot of candy," Mila says.

"I had to hide it. The stash lasted me two months," Hana admits. She reaches over to the table and presses the button so the arrow will spin.

It stops on Jase. "Hell yeah, give it to me, baby."

Kiss someone.

He darts up. "I'm all about sharing the love today." Taking hold of a squirming Mila, he plants a hard kiss to her lips. My eyebrows pop up when his lips tenderly move against hers before he pulls back.

Mila remains frozen, her eyes slowly blinking while Jase sends the arrow twirling again. It stops on Fallon.

Punch someone.

Without even thinking about who to punch, she lands one on Hunter's shoulder.

"Oww," I say on his behalf and reaching over, I rub his shoulder.

Fallon grins at me and leans over to the phone. The arrow stops on me, and I let out a groan.

Admit your love to someone.

My eyes lock on Mila in a split-second. "I love you so so so much."

She lets out a burst of laughter as I scramble off Hunter's lap to press the button again. While it spins, I quickly sink down to the floor and lean back against Hunter's legs.

Nice move, Jade.

The dare goes to Noah.

Kiss your enemy.

"Fuck, I love you all," he chuckles but then leans over to Kao and plants a kiss on his cheek.

"Dude, come on," Kao struggles, which only makes Noah kiss him again.

We all laugh at their antics while I remember how it felt when Hunter got that dare. Tingles rush over my skin, and absentmindedly I rub my hands over my arms.

"Are you cold?" Hunter suddenly asks, leaning down to me.

"Uh… no. I'm good."

Noah presses the phone, and when the arrow starts slowing, I duck down and almost become one with the floor. Everyone begins to laugh, and then Hunter reads out, "Give someone a lap dance."

I pop back up and see the dare written on the screen. "Oh, thank god I ducked."

Hunter grabs hold of my arms and lifts me to my feet. At first, I think it's so he can get past me, but then he steers me to the kitchen.

"What are you doing? It's your dare," I protest.

"Yeah, but I have to give someone a lap dance." He pulls one of the kitchen chairs into the open space between the two rooms and pushes me down in it.

"Noooo," I gasp, my eyes wide on him.

"I need music," he says, ignoring my protest.

Jase is up in a flash. "Give me a sec." He fiddles with the sound system, and then *Cruel Summer* by *Taylor Swift* begins to play.

I let out a groan and wildly shake my head.

Hunter begins moving, dancing backward as he nods his head to the beat. I let out a bark of laughter. But then he gets a freaking intense seductive look on his face, and when he bites his bottom lip, my laughter dries up like a puddle of water on a hot as hell day.

Hunter moves his hips in a way that has my mouth dropping open. He dances toward me and straddling my legs, he grabs hold of the chair behind my back and begins thrusting his pelvis at me.

My eyes shut so damn fast, and I struggle to keep from laughing again until I feel his breath against my cheek. My eyes snap back open, and the moment they connect with his blues, I'm a goner.

A sexy grin tugs at his lips as he pulls a little back, and then he yanks his shirt off in one swift move, leaving him only in his sweatpants.

Everyone begins to holler and clap hands while I stare at his chest. My eyes drop lower to where his abs flow into a scorchingly hot V.

Fuck-me-muscles galore.

273

You better move back if you don't want me drooling on you.

Of course, Hunter can't read my thoughts, and he continues to rub his chest up my body. I turn my face just in time to feel every perfect muscle glide over my cheek.

HOLY FUCKING HOTNESS.

When I turn my head back, I come face to face with his happy trail to the holy grail of ... what the hell am I thinking.

Don't look at his cock, Jade. Don't. Eyes up.

My eyes have a mind of their own, and they zero in on the bulge at the front of the loose hanging sweatpants.

It feels like I'm going to short-circuit, and I begin to blink faster.

Hot. Damn.

The song ends way too quickly, and climbing off me, Hunter pulls me up. I face plant against all his glorious muscles and happily wrap my arms around his waist.

Sigh… my new happy place.

"Don't you dare!" Mila suddenly shouts, popping my happy bubble. Pulling back, I crack up when I see Jase doing a pelvis thrust in her direction. It's nothing near as sexy as Hunter's was.

Hunter picks up his shirt, and I drink in the sight of his chest before the fabric falls over it.

"You have nothing on the show Jade just got," Mila taunts Jase.

"Oh yeah?" Jase leans into Mila and whispers something in her ear. When he pulls back, her eyes are wide, and her mouth is shut.

Hunter takes hold of my hand and pulls me back to the couch. He pushes me down in his seat, and then he sinks down at my feet, and I have to open my legs so he can sit between them.

God, this can't be my imagination. Does Hunter feel the same way about me?

Chapter 20

JADE

"Hell no," I say as Fallon throws a dress on my bed. "I'm never wearing anything like that again."

She wags her eyebrows at me. "It will get a certain someone's attention."

"Nope, I'm good, thanks." I wipe on some lipgloss and run my fingers through my hair. "Tonight, I'm sticking with my usual jeans."

Hana's eyes glide over me. "At least it's the tight ones."

"Everyone ready?" Mila asks from the door.

When I see the short dress on her, I let out a bark of laughter. "I see Fallon got her way with you."

She shrugs. "If you have the body, flaunt it, right?"

"Hell, yeah," Fallon yells.

"Let's go," Jase shouts from the front of the suite.

We all file out of my room and head out. When we spill out of the elevator on the ground floor of the dorm, I hang back with Kao, Mila, and Noah, waiting for Fallon to lead the way. Hana hooks her arm through Fallon's, and Jase falls in behind them.

Then Hunter grabs hold of my hand, yanking me to his side before he walks after them.

This is new.

He links his fingers with mine, and I quickly glance behind me, only to see three sets of toothy grins glaring back at me.

We split into two groups when we reach the cars, and I have no choice but to slip into the passenger seat when Hunter holds the door open for me. Jase and Mila climb into the back, and when Hunter slides behind the steering wheel, I quickly reach for my seat belt.

Pulling out of the parking, Hunter says, "We're not staying out late."

"Three am," Jase begins to negotiate.

By the time we reach Studio 9, Hunter and Jase agree on one am. I'm not sure I'm going to make it up that late. I'm already tired from all the fun we had this weekend, but not wanting to spoil my friends' night, I suck it up and pray for a second breath of energy.

I should've napped this afternoon instead of working on an assignment.

Climbing out of the car, I wait for Mila and walk with her into the club.

Human by *Rag'n'Bone Man* is thumping through the space as we walk to the VIP section. I sit down by the railing, so I have a view of the lower floor, and in need of a lot of sugar, I signal a waiter over and order a coke.

Hunter takes the chair next to me, and leaning closer, he asks, "Are you okay?"

"Yeah, just a little tired. I ordered a coke for sugar," I answer, giving him a wide smile.

"Let me know if I need to take you home," he offers.

Unable to resist, I lean into him and wrapping my arms around his neck, I press a kiss to his cheek and hug him. Pulling back, I grin, "I need to hug you more, or I'll never pay off my debt."

"In that case," Hunter chuckles as he pulls me back against his chest for another hug.

I close my eyes and breathe in his scent.

Damn, you smell sooooo good.

When he doesn't pull back, but instead, tightens his arms around me, I take full advantage of the moment and press as close to him as I can.

I feel the warmth from his body seep into mine, and it's only then I realize it's actually cold, and I should've brought a jacket. "You're so nice and warm," I mumble.

Pulling back, he asks, "You want my jacket?"

I shake my head and shift back into a comfortable position on my chair. "I'll go dance myself warm in a minute."

My coke comes, and I take a sip from the sugary goodness.

Hunter laughs at something Jase says, and I stare at his features.

When the hell did he get so handsome?

My eyes caress every line on his face, and I'm filled with an overwhelming feeling of awe for him.

I'm in love with you, Hunter.

Jase downs his tumbler of whiskey in one go and jumps up. "Let's go dance."

Hunter, Kao, and Fallon join Jase, and I watch them walk down to the dance floor.

"Why don't you go dance?" Hana asks me.

"I first need to finish my coke, or I'll fall asleep on the dance floor," I admit.

"You and me both," she replies, taking a huge sip of her own drink.

"Jase is such a player," Mila mumbles, her eyes focused on the lower floor.

I follow her line of sight and watch as Jase dances with a random girl. I glance over the immediate people around him, seeing Fallon and Kao. Frowning, I keep searching until I see Hunter sitting at a table with Nate and Jessica's group.

Hunter leans closer to Jessica and then laughs at something she says.

Damn, they look cozy.

I only manage the sight of them smiling into each other's eyes for another five minutes, then I get up. "I'm tired." I walk to the stairs and take them down as fast as I can. Glancing at Hunter one last time, I see Jessica lean into him, and he begins to lower his head. An intense wave of jealousy rocks me to my core. I've never felt anything like it before, and honestly, it's disturbing.

Fuck this shit. I'm done.

I rush out of the club, and only when I reach the sidewalk, do I realize I forgot my purse on the table, so I can't even call a cab. It's a thirty-minute walk at most. I can do it.

I stalk down the road, angry at myself for getting jealous when I have no claim to Hunter.

I thought…

Doesn't matter what I thought. I must've just imagined things. Hunter and I are just friends. At least I have that.

HUNTER

A curtain of dark silky hair falls over my shoulder, and then I hear Mila say, "I think Jade left."

"What?" I dart from the chair, and my eyes snap up to our table. Seeing only Hana and Noah sitting at it, I frown at Mila. "Seriously?"

"Yeah, and she left her bag. I thought she was just stepping out for fresh air, but she's been gone for ten minutes. I went to check, and there's no sign of her."

"Christ, Mila! You should've told me the second she left," I snap. I break out into a run, and when the cold night air rushes over me, worry claws up my spine.

I yank my car keys out of my pocket and run to the vehicle. Getting behind the wheel, the engine roars to life, and the tires squeal as I pull out of the parking area. I search along the road as I drive, hoping she just decided to walk home, and nothing bad happened to her.

Dark thoughts start to swarm in my head, making my heart race with fear. I'm about to have a panic attack from worry when I find her down the next street, heading in the direction of Trinity's campus. For a moment, I feel relief ripple through me.

If Mila didn't see Jade leave the club, Jade would be walking home alone. At fucking night! God knows what could've happened to her.

When the headlights of my car shine over her, she doesn't glance back, but instead, wraps her arms around her waist and keeps walking.

It's fucking cold outside, and the jeans and silk shirt she's wearing can't possibly offer her any warmth. I swerve the car around her then bring it to a stop a couple of feet ahead of her. Shoving the door open, I jump out.

Jade stops walking, her eyes on me as I stalk toward her. I stop an inch from bumping into her. Shrugging out of my jacket, I drape it around her shoulders.

Tilting her head back, she stares up at me with her eyes sparking with anger. Even in the darkness, I can see how pale her cheeks are from the cold.

"Left arm," I grumble, wanting to get her warm before we talk. Thankfully Jade listens, and I pull the sleeve up her arm, before moving the right. "Right arm." With the way too big fabric of my jacket covering her, I feel a little better but then growl, my voice low and hoarse, "Don't ever do that again,"

A hurt look ripples over her face as she snaps, "Fine."

"Why did you leave the club?" I ask, wanting to know what had her so upset she'd rather fucking walk home than ask for a ride.

Her features tighten, and her eyes narrow on me before she turns her glares to the road. "I'm tired and wasn't about to watch you and Jessica hook up."

Her words are a shock. A good one that makes all my anger fade like mist before the sun.

"Look at me." My eyes burn into the top of her head until she lifts her face and brings her simmering gaze to mine. "You got jealous?" I ask to make sure I'm not just hearing things.

Things I so desperately want to hear.

Fuck. Please say yes. Please. I can't keep pretending to be friends a minute longer.

Letting out a sigh, she shakes her head at me, then snaps, "Yes, Hunter. I got jealous."

Lifting my hands to her face, I frame her cheeks, my fingers splaying into her hair, and then I crush my mouth to hers.

I always thought a kiss was just a kiss.

Until Jade.

The second my lips touch hers, everything around us fades away. The cold. The street. The past.

Everything, but Jade.

My need to touch her, to make her mine is demanding, and filled with desperation. Jade parts her lips for me, and without a second's hesitation, my tongue sweeps inside, staking its claim.

I move one hand to the back of her neck, and I hold onto her like she's a lifeline.

Because she is.

She's always been my lifeline. Even during our fights, she was my everything. I'd rather spend a lifetime of fighting with Jade than a second without her fire, bringing warmth to my life.

Jade's hands come up, and she grabs hold of my biceps as her body presses into mine.

I nip hungrily at her bottom lip before plunging my tongue back inside the inviting warmth of her mouth.

Fuck.

The intensity of the moment crashes over me, and for a moment, I rock on my feet. I wrap my other arm around Jade's waist and pull her tightly against me.

I'm never letting you go again.

Never.

I pour the words into the kiss, and Jade pushes her body onto her tiptoes to get closer to me. Her fingers trail into my hair as she meets the strokes of my tongue with her own.

Never in a million years would I have guessed the passion behind our fights would lead to this moment.

This is why our fire never burned out but instead kept growing out of control. It was bound to destroy us or fuse us together.

I'm so fucking relieved it's the latter.

Our lips crush against each other, our bodies melting together. Jade clings to me as I move my hands down to her ass, and gripping hold of her, I lift her. She wraps her legs around my waist, her hands grabbing fistfuls of my hair as her tongue continues to lick the inside of my mouth.

The heat of her core pressing against my abs has my cock going hard as steel at record speed.

Fuck, I feel like superman.

Jade's always challenged me. She took me to the highest highs and lowest lows. My blood rushes through my body with want for this woman. Wanting her all to myself, I break the kiss and walk us to the car. "We need to get off the street."

Before I take you right here.

Jade nods, her breaths exploding over my skin as she ducks her face into the crook of my neck.

Reaching the vehicle, I drop her to her feet and open the passenger door. When I look down at Jade and see her swollen pink lips, I can't resist and press my mouth to hers. Just a single hard kiss because I'd much rather continue this in the privacy of our suite, instead of next to a street where anyone can see us.

When I have her seated in the passenger side, I reach for the seat belt and pull it around her. Once I have the belt clicked into place, I pull back and look at her. Her flushed cheeks have me leaning in and pressing another quick kiss to her mouth.

Silence fills the car on the drive back to the campus. I park the vehicle and climb out. Rushing around the front, I go to open the passenger door. When Jade gets out, I take hold of her hand and walk into our dorm.

When we step into the elevator, Jade glances up at me. "Just so I don't misunderstand things, what just happened?"

"We happened," I murmur, my voice still hoarse from the intensity between us.

"We happened?" she asks, confusion flitting over her features.

Not wanting to scare her off, I bite my declaration of love back. It might be too soon for Jade to hear. She needs time to get used to the idea of us as a couple.

Us.

A couple.

A smile begins to play over my face. "Yeah, *we*," I say as the doors slide open. I take hold of Jade's hand again and walk to our suite. Using my free hand, I swipe the keycard through the lock, and once we're inside and the door is closed behind us, I turn to face Jade and spell things out for her, "You and me. It's happening, Jade."

Chapter 21

JADE

Hunter wraps his arms around me and pulls me against his solid chest.

Hollllleeeeyyyyyy shit.

I can't believe what's happening right now. Hunter just kissed me like I've never been kissed before. My heart's a happy mess, but worry still blurs the edges of what could be my happily-ever-after.

"Are you sure?" I ask, concerned that he might just be reacting to residual emotions he has left from all our fights.

Turning his head, he presses a kiss to the crook of my neck. My eyes drift shut from the amazing tingles, caused by Hunter's lips on my skin.

"Yes," he breathes, his word fanning hot air onto my neck and sending a wave of goosebumps rushing over my body. "Are you sure?"

Am I?

I'm not sure if this is the best thing for us, but I'm certain it's what I want.

"I'm scared it will affect our friendship," I admit. I've screwed up so much where Hunter is concerned, that I don't want to risk losing him.

Hunter tilts his head and giving me a reassuring smile, he says, "Jade, if we could survive the last two years, we can survive anything."

I never thought of it that way. I've put us through hell, and Hunter never backed off. He stayed by my side every step of the way.

A relieved grin spreads over my face. "You're right."

His eyes soften as he stares at me for a while, then he whispers, "I want to kiss you."

Anticipation rushes down my spine. "Nothing stopped you before," I tease.

"Yeah," he gives me a sexy grin that has my stomach doing Olympic-worthy cartwheels. "Can I kiss you, Jade?"

I nod, my tongue darting out to wet my lips as the anticipation keeps growing.

Pushing against my body with his, Hunter steers me toward the living room. He sits down and taking hold of my hips, he tugs me forward. I climb onto his lap, resting a leg on either side of his lower body.

Hunter lifts his hands to my face and framing my cheeks, he pulls me toward him. "You're so fucking beautiful," he murmurs. One of his hands slides up behind me, and he wraps his fingers around the back of my neck.

Staring into his blue eyes, I'm caught in their depths. I'm highly aware of the feel of his body against mine, and a cloud of desire begins to drift over me.

"Can't you feel it too?" he asks, his eyes hooded on me.

"Damn, it's all I can feel. Kiss me already!" I wrap my arms around his neck, and not wanting to wait for another second, I fuse my mouth to his.

A deep groan escapes from Hunter's mouth as his lips begin to war with mine for control of the kiss. It's a new war — One I'll gladly lose for Hunter.

Sparks zap between us until the air feels electric. Heat sizzles through me, making anticipation and want whirl in my abdomen for this man.

My brain grows fuzzy, and my limbs heavy as Hunter continues to stroke the inside of my mouth with his skilled tongue. I love the taste of him and can easily become addicted.

When I need air, I break the kiss, but I don't pull away. Our breaths rush into each other, and our eyes lock.

I'm just about to kiss him again when the door opens.

"Fuck," Jase exclaims when he spots me on Hunter's lap. "Ookkaaayyy…" He tilts his head and frowns. "I've had way too much to drink to deal with this right now."

Mila bumps into his back and growls, "Move your ass. I need to pee."

"Hey," Hunter says, his voice a little hoarse. "You're back."

"Ahh, um…" Mila stutters while getting out of everyone's way. The group files into the suite, each one coming to a stop when their eyes land on Hunter and me.

"Finally," Fallon yells and rushing over to us, she throws her arms around us. "I'm so happy!"

"Are you guys a couple now, or is this a new way of fighting?" Jase asks.

My eyes dart to Hunter's, and not wanting to assume things, I leave it to him to answer Jase as I quickly move to sit next to him.

Hunter's eyes drift over my face, and a smile tugs at the corner of his mouth. With a sexy grin, he says, "We are definitely a couple."

Definitely. That's a solid yes, right?

With my eyes locked with Hunter's, our friends let out sighs of relief and hollers of joy.

Hunter pulls me into a hug, and when I feel his breath skim over my ear, he whispers, "I've fought so damn hard for you. No one will ever fight for you the way I will. Be mine?"

I'm overwhelmed with happiness and pull back a little as tears blur my eyes. I close them for a moment as I take deep breaths while I try to regain control over the happy mess inside of me.

When I open my eyes, it's to see a worried look on Hunter's face. Everyone is quiet as if they're waiting for a bomb to drop, and I can't blame them.

I clear my throat before I say, "You've always been my best friend, who stood by my side even when I tried to push you away. You're the man of my dreams, I never knew I was dreaming about." I take a deep breath and can't keep the tear from falling as I continue, "Hunter, I loved you during the happiest and darkest moments of my life. When my life fell apart, and I dealt the only way I knew how to, you took every blow."

A sob shudders through me, and it's all from realizing what I almost lost, and how much I have.

I blink the tears away so I can see his face. "I've always cared for you as a friend, but now... I love you with everything I have."

I don't care that I just laid my soul bare to Hunter, or that it happened in front of everyone. All I care about is that he knows how much he means to me. I never want a day to pass where Hunter doesn't know he's everything to me. He's the ground beneath my feet, the sun warming the coldest parts of my being.

Hunter takes a deep breath, a look of awe parting his lips, and then he yanks me against him, and our lips crash together. It's a hard but quick kiss, then he says, "Thank fuck." Another kiss. "God, you made me work my ass off." Kiss. "I'm never letting you go no matter how damn angry you get when we fight." Kiss. "Fuck." Kiss. "Finally."

When I begin to chuckle, he pulls back, and with his eyes smiling into mine, he whispers, "You were always meant to be mine, Jade. Love doesn't come close to describing how I feel about you." His fingers trail over my face. "Your fire… christ, you're fire. I live for it."

"God, I drank too much," Jase sniffles. "I can't believe I'm fucking crying." Disgusted, he wipes a tear from his cheek.

Mila and Hana are clinging to each other, happily smiling at us. Kao and Noah just grin at us.

But Fallon… Fallon's a sobbing mess, relief coming off her in waves, and I know Hunter and I fighting must've been so hard for her.

I reach over to her and give her hand a squeeze. "And we love you for always being the middle man… ah… woman between us."

"I'm just so glad," she says. "I feel like a proud mom whose kids finally made up."

I let out a chuckle and hug Fallon. Before I finish wrapping my arms around her, everyone piles onto us.

"Ahhh…. Get off," Fallon cries with laughter. "Y'all weigh a ton."

HUNTER

I've hardly slept as the morning sun begins to creep over the horizon.

I kept replaying the previous night in my mind, scared I'd wake up to it all being a dream.

Excitement bubbles in my chest as I throw the covers back. Walking into the ensuite bathroom, I reach into the shower and turn on the water. Stripping out of my sweatpants, I step under the spray and go through my routine.

Done, I dry myself off and wrap the towel around my waist. I brush my teeth and shave, then walk to my closet. My eyes scan over all the outfits, and wanting to look good, I grab a black pair of cargo pants, a button-up shirt to match and black leather brogues from Versace.

I roll the sleeves of the shirt up to my elbows as I head to my desk to grab my Rolex and strap it onto my wrist.

Pleased with how I look, I open my bedroom door and seeing Jade's is open, I glance inside. There's no sign of her, so I'm guessing she's at the gym.

Jase yawns as I walk into the kitchen. "You want some coffee?"

"Please." I sit down at the counter and grin at him. "I didn't sleep a wink."

He glares at me. "Then why do you look so awake. I'm dead on my feet. I swear I'm going to sleep through all my lectures."

"Serves you right for partying so hard," I taunt him.

He places a mug in front of me and drinks a huge gulp from his own before he says, "You being on cloud nine with love is too much so early in the morning." Finishing his coffee, he slumps back to his room.

I chuckle as I drink my own beverage, and I'm busy rinsing out my mug when the door opens. Jade comes in, her eyes on her phone as she takes the earphones out. She's sweaty and still catching her breath, but damn, the outfit looks fucking good on her.

"Morning," I say as I lean back against the counter.

Her head snaps up, and she stops dead in her tracks. "Morning."

I grin at her. "We're a couple."

She lets out a burst of laughter. "Yeah. So that happened last night."

I know she's not going to hit our relationship running. Jade has only had one boyfriend, and she needs time to get used to the idea.

Boyfriend.

My grin widens. "You're my girlfriend."

A blush creeps over her face, as she admits what I was just thinking, "I have to get used to the idea."

Pushing away from the counter, I walk toward her. Jade's eyes drift over me, and when I see them turn darker, I feel fucking pleased that she likes what she sees.

When I lift a hand to her face, she yanks away from me. "No, I'm all sweaty from the jog. Let me shower first."

I dart forward and framing her face, I plant a hard kiss to her mouth, then growl, "You all sweaty is one hell of a turn on."

"Hunter," she gasps, her face instantly turning a bright shade of red. She pulls free and darts around me, running for the safety of her room.

I let out an amused chuckle. Damn, I'm going to have so much fun teaching Jade what it's like to be in a relationship.

An adult one.

Chapter 22

JADE

This is happening.

Oh, God.

I sink down on my bed and stare at the floor. It's really happening between Hunter and me. Last night wasn't a dream.

Even though I opened up about my feelings, the relationship feels new and like I'm sailing in uncharted waters.

Mila comes in, followed by Fallon and Hana. They shut the door behind them and then join me on my bed.

"Tell us everything," Mila demands, wiggling her butt closer to me.

"You were there," I argue. "There's nothing more to tell."

"Oh, no," Fallon disagrees. "How do you feel? Are you happy? Are you sure about being with Hunter?"

I wait for her to stop rambling questions at me, then admit, "I love him, and I'm happy, but..."

"But?" Hana asks, her eyes widening at me.

"But... this is all so new," I admit. "With Brady, it took three months before we kissed. A peck on the lips. Our relationship consisted of holding hands and hugs."

Mila crosses her legs under her and glances at Fallon. "I have zero experience, so this is all on you."

"Why me?" Fallon gasps.

Mila gives her a wide-eyed look. "I thought you've... you know, done the deed."

Fallon grabs a pillow and whacks Mila with it. "I haven't."

"Okay," Hana sighs, "Let me get in here." She shifts closer then gives me a serious look. "What are you worried about?"

Mila and Fallon stare at Hana with surprise, but she ignores them, focusing all her attention on me.

I shrug. "What do I do? Do I hold his hand? When is the right time to initiate a kiss?" I cover my face with my hands and groan, "Don't even get me started on the sex part."

Hana reaches over to me and pulls my hands away from my face. "You hold his hand and kiss him whenever you want to, Jade. He's yours, and you are his. You don't have to wait for permission."

"What she said," Fallon chips in.

"Are you ready for sex, though?" Mila asks the million-dollar question.

"I wasn't really ready until it happened," Hana admits, which has our heads snapping in her direction. "Let it just happen naturally. You can't plan it, but if you do it with the person you love, everything will be fine."

"I have a ton of questions about the bomb you just dropped," Fallon says to Hana, then she turns her eyes to me. "Hana is right. If you feel you and Hunter are a sure thing, then just enjoy your relationship. Don't over-analyze everything."

"Yeah, I tend to do that," I admit.

Mila glances at her watch. "We need to get going, or we'll be late for class."

"Oh, shit!" I jump off the bed and run to the bathroom. "I still need to shower. I'll catch up with you all later."

I rush through my morning routine, and out of time, I leave my hair to air dry. It's going to be a curly mess, but I couldn't care less at this moment. I grab a hair tie and shove it onto my wrist, in case I need it later.

Dressed in a pair of jeans, a t-shirt, and a pair of sneakers, I dart out of the room. Remembering it was chilly this morning, I quickly rush back and grab a sweater from the back of my chair before hightailing it out of the suite.

I'm late for my first class, and with an apologetic glance at the professor, I sink down in the first open chair I can find.

My whole morning feels rushed as I dart from one class to the next. When it's time for lunch, I let out an exhausted sigh as I use the hair tie to tame my wild strands into a messy bun on top of my head.

An arm wraps around my waist, and I'm yanked against something solid. My eyes snap up, and it's just in time to see Hunter's face before he presses a kiss to my lips.

Students scurry around us, and for a moment, I think about the fact that we just went public with our relationship.

Like you ever cared what people thought.

I wrap my arms around Hunter's neck and pressing my mouth to his, I kiss him as if he's the air I need to breathe.

Because he is.

When I pull back, he gives me a sexy grin. "I could get used to that."

"Better than the hugs?" I tease him.

301

"Oh, way better." He takes hold of my hand and pulls me out of the building and into the sunlight.

"Please tell me we're going to eat," I say as I link my fingers with his.

"I asked the restaurant to prepare a basket for us." He smiles at me, and when he sees the question on my face, he explains, "It's a nice day out, and I thought we could have a picnic somewhere quiet so we can talk."

Talk? About what?

I'm still recovering from all the talking we did last night.

I don't say anything and let Hunter lead the way. We grab the basket, which I hope is filled with a lot of food, and begin to make our way down the trail I ran this morning.

I try to peek into the basket, but Hunter catches me and blocks my view with his body. "It's a surprise."

I pout at him, but then a smile wins out.

We reach the lookout point, and I sink to my butt, ready to eat.

Hunter sits down next to me and opening the basket, he unloads a world of goodness. He hands me a bottle of water, and I take a sip.

"We can talk after you've eaten. I'm scared you'll beat me up to get to the food," Hunter teases.

"Me? Never." I reach for a sandwich and take a huge bite. "Mmhhh…" I groan. "So good."

"Yeahhhhh." My eyes dart to Hunter's, and I see that he's staring at my mouth.

Wiping over it in case I have some crumbs stuck, I say, "Sorry, but you know I eat like a pig. I'm not about to become a salad girl."

He chuckles, shaking his head. "I don't expect you to."

I shove the rest of the sandwich into my mouth and close my eyes as I savor the buttery goodness. Opening the water bottle, I take a sip and then look at Hunter.

There's an intense expression tightening his features, his eyes locked on me.

"What?" I ask, placing the bottle on the grass.

"I wanted to talk first," he growls, "but… fuck…" The next second, Hunter moves over me, forcing me to lie down with his body hovering over me, and his mouth collides with mine.

Okay, kiss whenever we want to… I guess Hunter wants to… and yeah, I'm all for it.

When his tongue slips into my mouth, my thoughts scatter away, and I bring my hands to his jaw. I kiss him back, matching his intensity until we're both breathless.

When he breaks the kiss, he continues to lie half over me. His eyes drift over my face, and then he murmurs, "I wish you knew what you're doing to me."

Oh, shit. I thought we were in a good place?

Frowning, I ask, "Did I do something wrong?"

A slow smile spreads over his face as he shakes his head. "The opposite. You're doing everything right."

My frown only deepens as confusion sets in. "I'm not following. What am I doing to you, then?"

Hunter's head lowers again, and he presses a tender kiss to my lips. Pulling back, he admits, "You're driving me wild, Jade. It's hard to not touch you… and Christ… I just want to kiss you all the time."

A grin spreads over my face. "I'm not going to stop you."

"Good." He gives me a quick kiss before pulling me up in a sitting position, then he asks, "Are you really okay with us?"

I nod but still feeling apprehensive about certain things, I say, "I'm just not sure what to do. This is foreign territory for me."

Hunter tilts his head, a questioning look on his face. "What do you mean?"

Not wanting to bring up Brady to Hunter, I skirt around the truth, "I just have to get used to the idea."

Hunter's eyes sharpen on me, and I can literally feel him searching for the truth. "If you're not direct with me, I won't know what you're comfortable with and what not."

My shoulders slump, and I begin to pick at a blade of grass. "I didn't want to bring it up because you must be sick and tired of it, but I've only dated Brady." When Hunter doesn't look annoyed with me, I continue, "We only held hands and hugged, Hunter. This past couple of days, I've done more with you than I did with Brady."

I can feel my cheeks heating from having to admit how inexperienced I am to Hunter.

His eyes soften on me, and lifting a hand, he brushes a finger lightly over my cheek. "Then we'll take it slow. I never want to pressure you into doing something you're not ready for."

"I know you won't." I give him a thankful smile. "But..."

"But?" His eyebrow lifts in question.

"It's not that I'm not ready," I admit. I lower my eyes to my hands and swallow hard.

Just say it, Jade.

"Take your time," Hunter murmurs.

"It's just…" I swallow hard and force my eyes up to his. "I'm sure you're more experienced than me in a lot of things. I'm scared I won't meet your expectations."

Hunter moves closer to me and pulls me into his arms. With his hand on the back of my head, he holds me to his chest, and then he presses a kiss to the top of my head and says, "I have zero expectations, Jade. I just want to be with you. This isn't a race."

I wrap my arms around his waist, snuggling closer to him, and whisper, "I just never want to disappoint you again."

He rests his chin on my head. "As long as we're honest with each other, we'll be fine."

God, how did I ever get so lucky?

"You're a freaking saint," I admit, and it draws a chuckle from Hunter. "I make everything so damn hard."

"Yeah, you have no idea," he teases.

I pull back and playfully scowl up at him. "Now, you're looking for a beating. You're not supposed to agree with me."

Hunter begins to laugh. "But I meant it. You make everything hard, and I mean *everything*."

Oh shit. He's talking about his cock.

Oh. My. God.

My face lights up like the fourth of July, and I shove it against his chest to hide, which only makes him laugh more.

HUNTER

She's so fucking cute that I can't resist teasing her.

Yeah, I was referring to my cock, and it took her a while to catch on.

I'm surprised by what she told me, though. I was under the impression Jade and Brady were hot and heavy, seeing as they were ready to take the next step. But after what she just told me, I now know Jade's way more innocent than I thought.

With her leaning against my chest and my arms locked around her, I ask, "Just so we're on the same page, what's the furthest you've gone?"

Jade shoots up and turns her face toward the landscape, stretching out into the distance. "Oooh, and here I thought we were done talking about that part." She lets out a chuckle, still not looking at me. "With you, Hunter."

"We've only kissed," I clarify for her unless we did something I'm not aware of. Which is not a possibility at all.

Letting out a miserable sigh, she turns her body toward me and finally meets my eyes. "You knowwwww." Her eyes widen like she's trying to tell me to read between the lines.

Shaking my head, I say, "I've got nothing. What else did we do?"

"When I was straddling you at the gym," she whispers between clenched teeth, "You… uhm…" Shutting her eyes, she blurts out, "You got hard."

Laughter bursts from me when I finally realize what she's on about. "I wasn't sure you felt that."

"I did," she blurts out.

"Is that why you went to hide in your room?" I ask.

She nods again and then admits, "I was so damn shocked, I ended up calling Mamma G for help."

My mouth drops open. "You talked to Miss Sebastian about my cock?"

She lets out a burst of laughter. "That's one conversation I never thought I'd have with her."

Lifting my hand, I cover my mouth to keep from laughing. "Tell me what the two of you talked about."

"Nope." She shakes her head and presses her lips together.

"Tell me," I say as I begin to move toward her.

"Never." Her lips press shut again.

When I'm close to her, I lean in and press a kiss to her neck. "Please?"

"Huh-uh."

I let a breath fan out over her skin and watch as goosebumps form, then drop my voice low, "Pretty please."

"Oh shit, it's getting hard to say no," she groans.

I press another kiss to her neck and then trail my lips lightly up to her jaw, before breathing, "Tell me."

"I just asked her if it's normal for a guy to get hard," she admits.

"Hmmm." I keep trailing kisses over her skin until I reach her ear. "I only get hard when I see something I like."

"Oh," she gasps. "That's good."

I move back toward her mouth and stop an inch away from her lips. "What turns you on, Jade."

"This!" she blurts, her breaths speeding up. "This is definitely doing it for me."

"Yeah?" I groan.

"Definitely," she mumbles, and then she presses her mouth against mine. I let her control the pace of the kiss until she pulls back, and then she says with awe, "You're really good at it."

I sit back and grin at her. "Well, now I know how to get you talking. I've been doing it wrong all along."

"Arrogant ass," she sasses me before she picks up her water bottle.

"We should eat," I remind her and glancing at my watch, I say, "I have fifteen minutes before my next class."

She leans over and checks the time on my watch. "Shit, me too." Then she digs into the food like a starving person.

While we eat, we keep stealing glances at each other.

My heart is bursting with happiness. The picnic turned out much better than I hoped it would.

Chapter 23

JADE

As the days go by, I start to feel more comfortable around Hunter, and I can actually focus on my school work.

My life has done a total three hundred and sixty-degree turn. Thinking back to my first day at the academy, I never would've guessed just a couple of weeks later, I'd be in a relationship with Hunter.

Getting up from my bed so I can stretch my legs, I walk to the kitchen to grab a bottle of water.

"Are you almost done with your assignment?" Hunter asks from where he's sitting on the couch, watching TV with Jase, Kao, and Noah.

"Yeah. I just need to read through it," I answer. Taking a sip of water, I walk over to him. As I lean over the back of the couch, he tilts his head, and I press a kiss to his mouth.

When I straighten up again, he asks, "Can't you read through it tomorrow? It's getting late."

I lean over him again and taking hold of his wrist, I check the time. "Crap, I didn't realize it was one am already."

It's a Friday night, so the time doesn't really bother me seeing as I can sleep in.

Hunter gets up and walking around the back of the couch, he takes hold of my hand. "Night, everyone." And then he drags me to his room.

"Good night," I call out.

Not that the guys are even paying attention to us. They're all absorbed with the show they're watching.

When Hunter shuts the door behind us, I begin to feel nervous. "I still have to brush my teeth and put my phone on charge."

A slow grin spreads over his face. "Stop worrying. I just want to hold you while we sleep."

"I still need to do those things," I argue.

He opens the door again and leans against the jamb, crossing his arms over his chest. "Go do them. I'll wait."

I rush over to my room and run through my night routine. Making sure I've saved the document, I shut down my laptop before I glance down at the t-shirt and sweatpants I'm wearing.

My eyes dart to the door, and seeing Hunter still waiting for me, I walk to the bathroom to quickly take off my bra because there's no way I'm sleeping with one on.

Feeling a little self-conscious about not wearing one, I hunch my shoulders and cross my arms over my chest to cover myself.

Walking out of my room, I don't bother closing the door and quickly dart into Hunter's.

He shuts the door again, and this time locks it. "Finally, we get to sleep."

I wait for Hunter to drop down on the bed. He pulls the covers back for me, and I quickly climb on the mattress and lie down.

We're just going to sleep. There's nothing to worry about.

I keep chanting the words, but then let out a squeak when Hunter wraps his arm around my waist and pulls my body flush with his.

My eyes widen when he reaches over me and switches off the bedside lamp.

Oh. Oh. Oh. Shit.

But then he just tightens his hold on me, and placing his hand behind my head, he presses my face into the crook of his neck. "Night, babe."

A grin slowly spreads over my face.

Babe. I like that.

I wrap an arm around his waist and snuggling closer, I find a comfortable spot and close my eyes. Hunter's scent drifts around me, calming the nervous feeling I had.

I take a deep breath and smile against his skin.

Yeah, this is nice.

"Are you comfortable?" he murmurs.

"Yeah, and you?"

"Yeah."

There's a moment's silence, then Hunter asks, "Tell me what I missed during the past two years."

"Nothing much," I answer. I tighten my arm around his waist. "Just missed you."

"I missed you too," he whispers. "A lot."

HUNTER

Just hold her, Hunter.

I want to kiss her and touch her everywhere, but not wanting to push her too fast, I force myself to just hold her.

"How's your grandfather?" I ask, wanting to know more about the past two years.

"He's well. We're going to the ranch for Thanksgiving."

"Yeah? I'll miss you."

Jade chuckles. "I'll miss you too. It's only for three days. I'm looking forward to it. I haven't seen him since the summer break."

"I'm glad you'll get to spend some time with him. Is the ranch still your favorite place?"

Jade nods against my neck. "Yeah, I love it there. What are you doing for Thanksgiving?"

I take a deep breath, and when I begin to feel hot, I say, "I need to take my shirt off. Cuddling creates a shit load of body heat." I sit up and whip the fabric over my head, then drop it next to the bed. When I lie down again and wrap Jade up in my arms, she lets out a sigh as she snuggles her cheek to my chest. "You like that, hmmm?" I tease.

"Yeah," she sighs. "My favorite place."

"I thought the ranch was," I continue to joke with her.

"Was. I have a new favorite place," she mumbles.

315

I press a kiss to the top of her head and pull her body closer until she's half draped over me. "You're my favorite place too."

Jade kisses the skin over my heart.

Owing her an answer, I say, "Thanksgiving is at Hana's house this year."

"It's nice that your families take turns."

"Yeah," I agree. "I love how close we are."

"Are we going to tell our families about us?" Jade asks, and resting her chin on my chest, she glances up at me. Her eyes sparkle in the dark, and as much as I want to kiss her right now, I know if I start, I won't be able to stop.

"We can tell them when we're ready," I answer.

"Should we get them together and tell them in one go?"

I chuckle. "Good idea. That way, your dad can't kill me."

Jade begins to laugh, then says, "Don't be too sure about that."

Waking with Jade snuggled against my side is the best feeling ever.

Turning toward her, I wrap her in a tight hug and let out a happy sigh.

"Morning," she mumbles.

"Morning," my voice is still hoarse from sleep, and I clear my throat. "Let's spend the day here. I just want to hold you."

She wiggles out of my grasp and darts off the bed. "I'm first brushing my teeth and getting coffee. You want some?"

"Yeah," I answer with a chuckle.

When she rushes out of the room, I get up to go brush my own teeth. I quickly go through my morning routine and make sure I smell okay before I go to lie back on the bed.

I glare at my dick and grumble, "You better behave today."

Jade finally comes back with our coffees. She's changed into a pair of shorts and a clean shirt. My eyes are glued to her bare legs as she hands me a mug, and I almost drop it.

When she goes to close the door again, she asks, "What's the time? It looks like everyone's still asleep."

I check my watch, then say, "It's just gone past five." I Take a sip of coffee, then murmur, "I like the shorts."

She climbs on the bed. "Thanks. They're comfy."

We drink our coffee and keep stealing glances at each other. When we're done, and the mugs are on the bedside table, I reach out to Jade's thigh and draw lazy patterns on her skin.

"Should I bring my laptop so we can watch a movie?" she asks. "Or do you want to sleep some more?"

I shake my head and then darting forward, I push her onto her back. "I'd rather spar. Let's get some exercise in."

"Oh, yeah?" she asks, and then her hips buck up, and she uses all her strength to flip me onto my back.

Of course, I let her. I mean, why the hell wouldn't I want her on top of me.

Jade straddles my hips, and there's no way I can hide my hard as fuck cock from her as it presses against her. Her gaze widens slightly as she becomes aware of it, and for a split-second, her eyes drift closed.

Opening them again, I see confusion reflecting from her brown irises, and then she begins to move off me. Grabbing hold of her hips, I stop her and hold her in place.

What the fuck are you doing, Hunter?

Now's not the time to play with fire.

Scared as shit, she's going to panic and haul ass out of my room, I try to think of the right thing to say.

Fucker, this is not about you convincing her to stay.

"Are you uncomfortable?" I ask, wanting to know where her mind's at.

Jade shakes her head, and then she moves on me. I'm unable to bite back the groan, and relief fills me when Jade lets out a moan.

Her cheeks flush with embarrassment, and placing her hands on my chest, she tries to move to the side again, but I tighten my grip on her hips.

"Don't be embarrassed," I murmur, wanting to put her at ease. "Only stop if you're not ready and not because you're self-conscious."

Her eyes lock on mine. "Okay."

I lift my one hand to her face and brush my fingers over her blush. "It's okay, babe. Let's take this slow. It's supposed to be the fun part."

"Okay." A couple of seconds pass, then she admits, "It's just... I'm not good at this."

A gentle smile tug around my lips, and I praise her, "So far, you're doing a damn good job of getting me hard."

Her mouth twitches. "I'm not even doing anything."

"You're sitting on my cock, Jade. He's fucking happy right now."

She lets out a burst of laughter, and I feel pretty pleased with myself that I'm getting her to relax. Moving my hips, I slightly push up against her, and she must like the feeling because she moans from deep in her throat and grinds down on me. Tilting her head back, she closes her eyes.

Fuck. She's breathtaking.

"So… you've never…?" I ask, trying so hard to keep my voice even because her pushing down on me is enough to make my cock weep for more friction.

She glances at me for a second. When she realizes what I'm asking, her face lights up again with a blush, but then she admits, "I have a battery-operated boyfriend." Her eyes dart away from mine, and she bites her lower lip before continuing, "So I kinda took care of myself with that — god, this is soooo embarrassing." She ducks down, hiding her face against my chest.

Bringing my hands to her shoulders, I push her back up. "I need to know what you've done before, so I don't hurt you by accident." When she nods, I ask, "So, no oral, or anything else?"

She shakes her head, biting her bottom lip again, a mortifying look all over her face. "I guess my using BOB means that I'm technically not a virgin anymore."

"Bob?" I ask, a frown instantly darkening my face.

Jade lets out a burst of laughter, which I feel all the way in my cock, and it makes me twitch against her.

"Battery-operated boyfriend, aka my vibrator," she reminds me.

I let out a relieved sigh. "We need to get rid of BOB. I don't like competition." To clarify, I ask, "So, you have made yourself orgasm?"

Nodding, she laughs again, and it causes her whole body to rock against me.

Fuck, that feels so good.

I push up against her again, drawing another moan from her, and I swear I'll lose my load if she makes that sound again.

Moving my hands back to her thighs, I slowly inch my way up. Our eyes are locked, hooded, and burning with desire.

Whenever we get to the point where we have actual sex, planets are going to fucking collide, because just rubbing myself against her, has me almost coming in my pants.

Slowly, we begin rocking together, and it feels so incredible that it steals my breath.

Fuck, we're dry humping, and it feels better than any sex I've had before. Not that I've been with hundreds of girls. There's only been two, and they will never compare to Jade on her worst day.

"Shit," Jade whispers as she continues to rock on top of me. My hands slide higher until I grip hold of her ass.

My fucking cock is so hard right now, I'm afraid I won't last much longer.

"Kiss me, Jade," I whisper, my voice hoarse from all the strain. She leans over me and softly presses her mouth to mine. Bringing my one hand up, I clasp the back of her neck and press her mouth harder down on mine.

The kiss quickly turns to licks and sucks, and our breathing grows heavier.

God, she feels so fucking incredible.

Our movements speed up until we're both frantic. When Jade's practically panting against my mouth, I tighten my grip on her ass and rub my cock shamelessly against her fabric-covered pussy.

"Shit, Hunter!" Her breathing stalls, and she freezes on top of me as her orgasm hits. My eyes lock on her face, and watching her come undone is so fucking erotic there's no way I can stop myself from finding my own release.

Losing my load in my pants is a first for me, but it's the hottest experience I've ever had.

Chapter 24

JADE

Listening to the shower running, I sit on the edge of the bed while waiting for Hunter to get out.

Holy shit!

Yeah, we just did that.

Oh, my god.

Yep, mind officially blown.

I can't wipe the grin from my face, and when Hunter steps out of the bathroom, my jaw literally drops. He's only wearing sweatpants, and they're sitting pretty low on his hips, giving me a perfect view of his fuck-me-muscles.

With a towel in his one hand, he catches the last of the drops still on his chest, and then he throws it to the side.

"Babe, if you keep looking at me like that, I'll have to go take a cold shower," he teases me.

"But… damn," I sigh, unable to tear my eyes away from his abs. Wanting to touch him, I quickly shove my hands under my butt.

You've just ridden Hunter like a damn horse. Contain yourself, hussy.

Hunter comes to sit next to me, his bare arm pressing against mine, and then he wipes at the corner of my mouth. "You're drooling."

I let out a burst of laughter and slap him against his chest. My hand gets a mind of its own and begins to rub over the hard planes my eyes have been feasting on. "If you don't put on a shirt, I'm just going to slobber all over you," I say, not even pretending that I'm not affected by all his hotness.

I pull my hand back and tilting my head, I let my eyes rove over him again. "If I lick you, that will mean you're mine, right?"

His shoulders begin to shake with laughter. "If you lick me, I'm going to lose the little control I have left and fuck you senseless." Then he turns serious and asks, "You want to talk about what happened before I went to shower?"

"I'm good," I mutter, not wanting to talk about the orgasm that blew my mind. It feels too personal.

"And by good, do you mean the orgasm was good?" he continues to ask the most mortifying questions.

"Hunter," I whine, pushing out my bottom lip.

"Jade," he groans, leaning closer to me until I can feel his breath on my neck. He presses a soft kiss to my skin before pulling back. "I'm actually surprised that you're not vocal about the whole experience. Usually, I can't get you to shut up."

"Are you telling me I talk too much?" I ask, pulling back so I can see his face.

"No." He grins at me. "I love the fact that you always speak your mind, so it's making it hard to read your thoughts right now."

He presses another kiss to my neck, and then lightly blows hot air over my skin, making goosebumps rush over my body.

Taking hold of my hips, he pulls me onto his lap. I can feel how hard he is, and I quickly bite down on my bottom lip, trying my best to not ride him again.

Hunter pushes up against me, and feeling how much he wants me draws a moan from me.

Yep, we're doing this again.

The first time was epic, so I'm all for a second ride.

He kisses my neck again, then continues to trail up to my jaw. I turn my face to him, and we stop with our lips so close to each other, we're breathing the same air.

"Fuck, Jade," he groans. "It's really hard to keep my hands off you."

"It's not the only thing that's hard," I tease, grinding down on him to make my point.

Oh, look at me getting all brave.

Surprise flickers in his blue eyes before they begin to burn with desire. "Mmm... I'm creating a monster, aren't I?"

I nod and bringing my hands to his face, I brush my fingers lightly over his jaw while my eyes caress every inch of his features, and I whisper, "When did you become so handsome?" Moving my hands down to his shoulders, I revel in the feel of his muscles beneath my fingers. I keep going down to his rock-solid chest before I trail a single finger over his perfect abs. "Damn, you're soooo hot," I admit to him.

I press a kiss to his shoulder as my hands go into uncharted territory, caressing the stretch of skin right beneath the band of his sweatpants.

"Jade." There's a tone of warning in his voice, and it makes me freeze.

Glancing up at him, I ask, "Do you want me to stop?"

He shakes his head but then answers, "No, but if you keep going, I really won't be able to stop. You're pushing my limits."

Leaning in, I press a kiss to his chest, then I whisper, "What if I don't want you to stop?"

Hunter grabs hold of my butt and lifting me, he flips me over, so I'm lying on his bed. His body towers over mine, and the sight alone is enough to draw a needy moan from me.

His hands move to my hips, and taking hold of the fabric of my shorts, his eyes lock on mine. "Are you sure you want to take the next step?"

I nod, and it's all it takes for Hunter to pull my pants and panties down in one move. His head dips down, and he presses a kiss to my stomach, and then he moves lower and lower until he gets to the part that has my face going up in flames.

I never thought it would be so hard to be naked in front of a man. What the hell was I thinking at sixteen? In hindsight, I now know I was nowhere near ready for sex back then.

I lay still, too scared to move a muscle as I wait for Hunter to say something, or to move, or to do whatever he was going to do next.

"God, Jade," he exhales, and then I feel the tip of his finger brush over my curls. "You're so fucking beautiful,"

I watch him take hold of my legs. He raises them over his shoulders and then his mouth is on me, hot and desperate. Instantly my ass bows off the bed as intense feelings I've never experienced before bombard the apex between my thighs.

"Holy... shit," I manage to moan. I try to grab hold of something as Hunter's teeth nip over my sensitive flesh, licking and sucking until I grab hold of his hair. "God, Hunter!"

It feels like my insides detonate, setting my whole body on fire as pleasure paralyzes me.

"Christ, Jade. You taste so fucking good."

I grip his hair tighter, and I'm pretty sure I'm about to remove a chunk. Hunter pulls back and shoving his own sweatpants down his legs, it has my panting breaths stalling for a moment as I stare at his hardness.

Holy, huge cocks. Hunter is bigger than my vibrator, and I had trouble getting it inside me.

Hunter places his hands on my stomach and begins to push the fabric of my shirt up. Sitting up, I help him pull it over my head. Before I can lie back down, his hand moves to my back, and he unclasps my bra.

A second wave of self-consciousness hits as he bares my breasts to him. I'm just about to cover myself with my arms, when Hunter growls, "Don't you dare. Keep still and let me look at you."

Not moving a muscle, I keep stealing glances at his face as his eyes roam over my naked body. He shakes his head, and for a second, my stomach dips with dread, but then he whispers, "A fucking masterpiece."

He brings his hand to my chest and lightly brushes a finger over the swell of my breast.

When he slips an arm under me, and he shifts me up to the middle of the bed, I begin to get nervous.

Shit, this it.

I'm about to have sex for the first time.

With Hunter.

Shit.

What if I suck at it?

"Jade." The sound of my name yanks me back to the present. "Get out of your head," Hunter says as he lies down on top of me.

I can feel his hardness, which I'm pretty sure is going to have one hell of a struggle fitting inside of me, resting between my legs.

"Ahh…" I don't know how to tell Hunter we might have a problem.

"Do you want to stop?" he asks, lifting his upper body from mine and resting on his right arm.

"It's not that I want to stop," I say, and then I squeeze my eyes shut and just power through, rambling, "I don't think you're going to fit. You're much bigger than my vibrator, and I can't even get that thing to go in all the way."

When Hunter doesn't say anything, I peek at him through one eye. He's looking at me with a huge grin spread over his face, as if I've just made his damn day, instead of telling him we have a problem.

Opening both my eyes, I ask, "You heard me, right?"

Hunter nods, still looking like a cat that got all the cream. "I'm totally enjoying the compliment, right now. Give me a minute."

I slap his shoulder and scowl at him. "I'm serious."

He moves back over me and presses a kiss to my lips. "Don't worry about me fitting. That's my job."

"Job? You make it sound so clinical," I complain. This experience is going downhill fast.

"Sorry, babe." He gives me another kiss and pulling back, he says with a low timbre to his voice, "Just relax and let me love you."

I push my bottom lip out, still worried about my poor vagina. "Just don't split me in two. I'm kinda attached to my vagina."

He begins to chuckle. "You're so damn cute when you're nervous."

"I can't help it. I haven't done this before," I explain, feeling inexperienced and stupid.

"By the way, is your vagina on the pill?" he asks, drawing a burst of laughter from me. I nod, which has him asking another question, "Are you okay with me being bare?"

My eyes flit away from his, and I nod.

"Look at me," he whispers.

Focusing on Hunter's blue eyes, I suck in a deep breath to calm down.

He keeps staring at me for a long moment until I can see the love he feels for me shining from his eyes. It's like I'm being put under a spell, and when his lips come down on mine, I'm swept away by his tongue exploring my mouth. I kiss him back with the same heat until our bodies begin to rub against each other, and our hands start to wander.

My palms take in the feel of his muscular back until I reach the dip of his butt, then my nails get involved, and I dig them into his firm skin.

Hunter's hand finds my breast, and he begins to knead my flesh. We're both a panting mess, but our kiss goes on and on until our lips are tingling. When we finally pull apart, our eyes lock, and there's so much intensity in Hunter's blue gaze, there's not a doubt in my mind that he loves me.

I never want to go another day without him knowing that he's my world. "Hunter, I am so in love with you. You are everything I never knew I needed. I don't know how I survived the past two years without you."

"I was always there, Jade," he says. "I never stopped loving you."

This time when our mouths meet, there's so much passion in his kiss, it drugs me the same way our first kiss did. I'm only aware of the feel of his body against mine. I can only smell his masculine scent, and the lingering body wash he used. I can only hear his breaths, and I live for each one of them.

This moment between us feels intimate, almost sacred. It's something I never want to share with anyone but Hunter.

He positions himself at my opening, his weight held up with his right forearm. When I feel pressure from where he's pressing into me, my eyes fly to his, and I latch onto the love I see in his gaze.

He pulls back, and with gentle rocking movements, he keeps going deeper until he's fully sheathed inside of me.

Hunter is inside me. My Hunter. My love. My life.

I'm so glad I got to give this moment to him.

"Perfect fit," Hunter whispers as he lowers his head to mine and claiming my lips, he continues to devour me while giving me a moment to adjust to him.

I never should've doubted him because everything he does is so goddamn right, it feels like my body is going to implode from pleasure when he begins to move.

The sounds of our pelvises coming together create a symphony of love around us as pressure builds in my abdomen. Just when I think I can't take it anymore, it rushes through my body, tearing a moan from me. With my body suspended beneath Hunter's powerful one, I can only manage a silent cry. Feelings I've never felt before turn my body to nothing but jello.

"Fuck, Jade," Hunter growls low in his throat and thrusting twice more, he pushes so hard into me it sends residual pleasure rippling over me. I feel his body shudder against mine and drink in the sight of Hunter finding his release in me.

How was I so blind? The most beautiful human being was right in front of my eyes all this time.

Overcome with emotion for this man who went through hell for me, a tear sneaks from my eye. Hunter catches it with a kiss and pressing his face into my neck, he whispers, "I love you so much, Jade."

I know, Hunter. You've shown me just how much, over and over. I'll never doubt you again.

HUNTER

So much for being patient.

Not that I regret a single moment.

After we get dressed, and we lie down, I pull Jade against me and press a tender kiss to her mouth.

"Thank you," I whisper against her temple as I get comfortable.

"For what?" she asks, and turning her face, she glances up at me.

"For letting me be your first." My eyes bore into her, and I hope she can see how much it means to me.

A soft smile plays around her mouth. "I'm glad it was you."

"Yeah?" Thank, fuck. I was worried, seeing as all our problems started when I stopped her and Brady.

Jade must read the concern in my eyes because she sits up and turns her body to face me. There's a flash of sadness in her gaze, then she says, "I'll always love Brady, and I'll never forget him, but I love you in a way I never thought I could care for another person. You were right, Hunter. I wasn't ready back then. I was a stupid sixteen-year-old who thought I knew everything." She lets out a sigh. "Boy, was I wrong."

"It's okay," I murmur, and reaching out to her, I take hold of her hand and link our fingers.

She takes a deep breath, and her eyes begin to shine as she stares into mine. "I'm glad it was you, Hunter. Everyone says you don't get to choose who you love, that it just happens and you have to go with the flow, but they're all wrong. My heart chose you long before my head knew it. I chose you every day I fought with you. I chose you every time I said no to a guy asking me on a date." A breath ripples over her lips, and her voice cracks, "I chose you every second of every hour for the past seven hundred and thirty days, and I'll keep choosing you for the rest of my life."

Pulling her to me, I hug her hard against my chest. Overcome with emotion, I need a minute to regain my composure. I press kisses to her hair, and I try to even my breathing.

Finally, I whisper, "I'll never do anything to make you regret your decision."

"I know," she whispers, sending warmth from her breath over my chest. "I don't deserve you, but I'll treasure you."

I close my eyes and wrap my arms tighter around Jade. We cling to each other, our hearts beating the same rhythm.

"I love you, Bean," I whisper.

Lifting her head, she grins up at me. "I love you, Hunter."

The Epilogue

HUNTER

Jade and I decided to tell our parents we're together before Thanksgiving.

"Everything's going to be okay, right?" Jade asks again, her leg jumping where she's sitting in the passenger seat.

Reaching over, I place my hand on her thigh. "Everything will be fine," I reassure her. "Let me tell them."

"But my dad," she argues.

"Let me handle it, Jade." I glance at her before I steer the car up Uncle Rhett's driveway.

I recognize Dad's car and glancing at the other vehicle, I ask, "Is that Miss Sebastian's car?"

"Yeah, she knows everything, so she'll be able to play peacekeeper if things get out of hand."

I let out a chuckle. "It was clever of you to invite her." I switch off the car and leaning over to Jade, I press a kiss to her lips. "Let's do this."

Climbing out of the car, I jog around the front and open the door for Jade. When she gets out, I take hold of her hand, and together we walk to the front door.

When Jade pushes it open, she tries to pull her hand from mine. When I don't let go, her eyes dart up to me. "I'm not going to hide how I feel, Jade. I'm holding your hand," I state, the tone of my voice leaving no room for arguing.

"Okay." She sucks in a deep breath, and then we walk into the house.

When we enter the living room, everyone's eyes snap to us. "Hey," I say, and I have to clear my throat before I continue, "Thanks for meeting us here."

"Christ, please tell me you're not pregnant," Uncle Rhett explodes.

Jade lets out a burst of air, and her mouth drops open. "Dad, noooo! That's not why we asked you here."

Uncle Rhett let's out a relieved sigh, slumping back against the couch. "Thank God. Here I thought you asked Hunter to save your ass in case we wanted to kill you."

"No. Noooo. No," Jade repeats, shaking her head. "That's not the reason."

Pulling her hand from mine, she goes to hug my mom and dad. I walk to Uncle Rhett and shake his hand before giving Aunty Evie and Miss Sebastian a hug each.

I take hold of Jade's hand, and I pull her down next to me as I take a seat. Dad tilts his head and narrows his eyes at me. "Well, I never saw that coming."

"What?" Uncle Rhett asks.

"They're dating," Mom answers.

Uncle Rhett's head snaps in my direction. "You're dating my daughter?"

I give him an anxious smile, as I explain, "We just started dating."

Uncle Rhett stares at me, his face void of any expression. Not breaking eye contact, I wait for a reaction.

Then Miss Sebastian jumps up. "Rhett Daniels! Don't just sit there like a dead fish out of water. Say something."

Uncle Rhett shoots her a glare then mutters, "I'm still processing the fact that my little girl is living under the same roof as Hunter." He pulls a worried face. "And they're dating." Looking stunned, he stares at the floor. "Jade should move back home."

"Daddy," Jade gasps.

I glance at my father, and he gives me a reassuring smile.

"Uncle Rhett," I begin, and his eyes instantly snap to mine. "I love Jade, and I'll never do anything to hurt her."

He pulls a face as he considers my words. "I know, Hunter." Not looking happy, he continues, "I don't like the idea of the two of you living together."

"It's no different from me living with Jase, Noah, and Kao," Jade argues.

"Yeah?" Uncle Rhett gives Jade a sardonic look. "You're not kissing them."

I try to hide my smile, but I fail miserably, which has Uncle Rhett glaring at me. "I'm still not happy."

"Oh, Rhett, hush," Aunty Evie says as she gets up and walking over to us, I quickly rise to my feet. She wraps me in a hug, and says, "I'm glad it's you, Hunter. I was so worried when you kept fighting with each other. I can't tell you how relieved we are to hear you've made peace."

"That's not the kind of peace I had in mind, Evie," Uncle Rhett complains.

"Ignore him," Miss Sebastian says as she comes to hug me as well. "Just take good care of my god-baby, or I'll tan your bedazzled ass with my diamond-studded belt."

I choke as I try not to laugh, but when Dad cracks up, I'm unable to keep it in.

Miss Sebastian lovingly pats my cheek, then she darts past me. "My god-baby finally got her own chunk of hunk."

My gaze turns back to Uncle Rhett, and when he gets up, I quickly walk to him. "I'll take good care of Jade. I promise."

A grin spreads over his face, and he pats me against the shoulder. "I'm just fucking with you. We all knew you were dating the instant you asked us to meet here."

My lips part, and then I just shake my head. "You had me there for a while. Good one."

Dad gets up and comes to stand by us. "I'm not gonna lie, the bets were up in the air whether you'd kill each other or finally admit your feelings."

"Who won?" I ask, giving them all a playful glare.

"We did," Mom says as she wraps her arm around Auntie Evie's waist.

"Yeah," Dad admits. "Your Mom never doubted for a minute that the two of you would sort out your shit."

"How did you know, Mom?" I ask, a burst of love filling my heart because she never doubts anything I do.

"You're my son, Hunter, and even though you inherited your father's stubborn streak, you got my patience."

"Patience my ass, Hunt," Dad grumbles at Mom, calling her by her maiden name, which is also his nickname for her. "You gave me hell when we first started dating."

"Because you deserved it," Mom snaps back.

I let out a chuckle because I know where this argument is heading. Turning my attention back to Uncle Rhett, I hold out my hand. "So, you're okay with us dating?"

He shakes my hand and then pulls me in for a hug, whispering, "I'm more than okay with it, Hunter. I know how hard you fought for Jade."

I wrap my arms around him, hugging him back. "Thanks, Uncle Rhett."

JADE

When Aunty Kingsley sits down next to me, Mom and Mamma G leave me to fend for myself as they escape to the kitchen. My eyes dart to the sliding door leading out to the veranda where Hunter is grilling steaks with our fathers.

Suck it up, Jade.

I give Aunty Kingsley a nervous smile, and ask, "Are you really okay with us dating?"

"Before I answer that question, I have something to say," she begins.

I meet her eyes, staring into the same blue irises as Hunter's, and prepare myself as best I can for whatever's coming.

"You went through something awful, Jade, and Hunter was there for you. I just want to make sure you really love my son, and that you're not just grateful for what he's done."

I shake my head and have to take a deep breath when I'm overcome with emotion.

Who knew it would be so intense talking to Hunter's mom.

I clear my throat and shake my head again. "I love him, Aunty Kingsley. So, so much." My eyes lower to my lap for a moment before I meet hers again. "I wouldn't have survived it without him. I admit that. But what I feel for him… it's because he's the most amazing man I know. He's my sun, and without him, my life would be a frozen wasteland." I take a moment to gather my thoughts, not wanting to screw this up. "I… I just love him so much."

Aunty Kingsley stares at me for a long moment, then she whispers. "Please don't hurt him again."

A lump swells in my throat, and I swallow hard on it as my tears blur. "Never again. I promise I'll do everything in my power to make Hunter happy."

"Just love my baby," she says, her voice straining with unshed tears.

"I will. I'll love Hunter with all of my heart," I promise.

Aunty Kingsley reaches over, and I quickly hug her back. We hold onto each other for a while, then she whispers, "I'm so happy you're dating Hunter."

"Is everything okay in here?" Hunter suddenly asks.

Aunty Kingsley and I pull apart, and she nods at him, giving him a loving smile. "Everything's fine."

His eyes dart between us, and then he frowns. "Why do I see tears?"

"Just because," I mumble as I wipe my cheeks dry. "I'm allowed to get emotional when I speak to your mom."

Walking over to me, Hunter leans over and presses a kiss to my mouth, then he moves over to Aunty Kingsley, and he presses a kiss to her forehead. "My two favorite women. I'm such a lucky man."

And that's all it takes for Aunty Kingsley and me to start crying again.

HUNTER

Sitting outside by the fire, I smile as my eyes scan over my family. When my gaze drifts over Uncle Rhett, Aunty Evie, and Miss Sebastian, the smile only grows bigger.

And then there's the moment old friends become a part of that family.

Fuck, I'm such a lucky bastard.

I tighten my grip on Jade's hand and glancing at her, I wink. Seeing her glass is empty, I ask, "Can I get you more coke?"

She shakes her head and leans her cheek against my shoulder. "I'm so happy."

"Me too, babe."

Miss Sebastian gets up and pulls a wrapped package from her purse. "I got you a congrats-on-finally-getting-your-bedazzled-asses-together gift," she says as she hands me the box.

"You shouldn't have," Jade says as she sits up again. Her eyes dart to mine, "Open it already."

"So damn bossy," I mumble as I tear at the paper.

Dad chuckles.

When the wrapping comes off, I freeze. A second later, I crack up with laughter while staring at the box of Trojan condoms.

"I got you the pleasure pack," Miss Sebastian says, wagging her manicured eyebrows at me.

I can't stop laughing, and when Jade reads the front of the box, she gasps, "Oh. My. God. Nooooooo!" Grabbing the condoms from me, she quickly sits on it.

"Pleasure pack?" Uncle Rhett asks Miss Sebastian.

"Rather safe than sorry," she shrugs. "Do you want little Hunter's and Jade's running around here?"

"What the fuck?" Uncle Rhett complains, shaking his head, then he barks, "You gave them condoms?"

Dad can't hold his laughter any longer, and he cracks up.

I try to reach under Jade to pull the box out, but she slaps at my hand, and hisses, "Don't, Hunter." Her face is on fire as she hides her reaction behind a hand from her dad.

"It's okay," I chuckle, and reaching for her hand, I pull it away from her face. "Let me have the box. I want to make sure Miss Sebastian got the right size."

"Oh, don't you worry, my little chunk of hunk," Miss Sebastian says, winking at me. "I got extra large."

"Oh, god. Kill me now," Jade groans.

Through a fit of laughter, I manage to pull Jade into my arms so she can hide her face in my chest.

"Time for apple pie," Aunty Evie says as she gets up, and it effectively changes the topic of discussion to who's getting the bigger slice.

When our parents and Miss Sebastian head into the house to fight about the pie, Jade quickly yanks the box from under her butt. "Let's go put it in the car before I die from embarrassment."

We link our hands as we walk around the side of the house, and reaching the car, I quickly unlock the passenger door. Jade tries to shove the box under the seat, but when it's too big to fit, she leaves it lying on the floor.

I lock the door again and shove the keys in my pocket. Before Jade can walk back, I grab hold of her arms and pull her to me as I lean against the car.

"I think that went okay," I say as I stare into her eyes.

A smile splits over her face, and she nods. "More than okay."

"Yeah." My eyes drop to her mouth and press a quick kiss to it. "I'm just glad your dad's okay with us dating."

"Me too." Rising up on her toes, she presses a kiss to my lips. When she pulls back, her gaze is filled with emotion. "I love you, Hunter."

I bring a hand up to her face and brush my fingers over her cheek. "You have no idea how much I love you."

Jade shakes her head lightly. "I do know, Hunter. Trust me, I know." Her lips touch mine, then she whispers, "You went to war for me, and you won." Her eyes caress my face. "You've given me new dreams. A future filled with hugs, love, and seeing your smile. You gave me back my life."

Framing her face, I crush my mouth to Jade's, and I kiss her with everything I feel. When I pull back, my voice is filled with emotion as I say, "A future with you. God, I'm so fucking lucky."

The End.

Want to read where it all started?

Go 1 Click HEARTLESS.

And when you're done with the Enemies To Lovers Series, follow it up with Trinity Academy.

If ever life gets too much, please reach out to someone or call a suicide crisis line near you.

List of suicide crisis lines worldwide:

https://en.wikipedia.org/wiki/List_of_suicide_crisis_lines

The Heirs

Reading order of future releases:

Coldhearted Heir
Novel #1
Hunter Chargill (*Mason and Kingsley's son*)
&
Jade Daniels (*Rhett & Evie's daughter*)

Arrogant Heir
Novel #2
Jase Reyes – (*Julian & Jamie's son*)
&
Mila West – (*Logan & Mia's Daughter*)

Defiant Heir
Novel #3
Kao Reed (*Marcus and Willow's son*)
&
Fallon Reyes (*Falcon & Layla's daughter*)

Loyal Heir
Novel #4
Forest Reyes (*Falcon & Layla's son*)
&
Aria Chargill (*Mason & Kingsley's daughter*)

Callous Heir
Novel #5
Noah West (*Jaxson & Leigh's son*)
&
Carla Reyes (*Julian & Jamie's daughter*)

Sinful Heir
Novel #6
Tristan Hayes (*Carter & Della's son*)
&
Hana Cutler (*Lake & Lee's daughter*)

Tempted Heir
Novel #7
Christopher Hayes (*Carter & Della's son*)
&
Dash West (*Jaxson & Leigh's daughter*)

Forbidden Heir
Novel #8
Ryker West (*Logan & Mia's son*)
&
Danny Hayes (*Carter & Della's daughter*)

SPIN-OFF STAND ALONE

Black Mountain Academy Series

Not My Hero
Colton Lawson's story.

Trinity Academy

FALCON
Novel #1
Falcon Reyes & Layla Shepard

MASON
Novel #2
Mason Chargill & Kingsley Hunt

LAKE
Novel #3
Lake Cutler & Lee-ann Park

JULIAN
Novel #4
A Stand Alone Novel
Julian Reyes (*Falcon's Brother*)
&
Jamie Truman (*Della's Sister – Heartless*)

THE EPILOGUE
A Trinity Academy Novella

Enemies To Lovers

Heartless
Novel #1
Carter Hayes & Della Truman

Reckless
Novel #2
Logan West & Mia Daniels

Careless
Novel #3
Jaxson West & Leigh Baxter

Ruthless
Novel #4
Marcus Reed & Willow Brooks

Shameless
Novel #5
Rhett Daniels & Evie Cole

False Perceptions
Novel #6
A Stand Alone Novel
Hayden Cole *(Evie's Dad)*

Connect with me

Newsletter

FaceBook

Amazon

GoodReads

BookBub

Instagram

Twitter

Website

About the author

Michelle Heard is a Wall Street Journal, and USA Today Bestselling Author who loves creating stories her readers can get lost in. She resides in South Africa with her son where she's always planning her next book to write, and trip to take.

Want to be up to date with what's happening in Michelle's world? Sign up to receive the latest news on her alpha hero releases → NEWSLETTER

If you enjoyed this book or any book, please consider leaving a review. It's appreciated by authors.

Acknowledgments

Sheldon, you're my everything.

To my alpha and beta readers, Sherrie, Sheena, Allyson. Kelly, Elaine, Sarah, and Leeann – Thank you for being the godparents of my paper-baby.

Candi Kane PR - Thank you for being patient with me and my bad habit of missing deadlines.

Sybil – Thank you for giving my paper-babies the perfect look.

To my readers, thank you for loving these characters as much as I do.

A special thank you to every blogger and reader who took the time to take part in the cover reveal and release day.

Love ya all tons ;)

Made in United States
Troutdale, OR
11/18/2024

24991740R00199